THE
ATHENA
MECHANISM

The optimum solution is sometimes
the one that is hardest to take

THORNTON ALLEN

To the victims, the collateral damage, created when politicians decide that the end always justifies the means.

Acknowledgements

With thanks to those who put me in a position to write and publish this book. In particular, my design team including JD Smith Design (Cover and formatting) and Lisa Roberts (Photographic).

CHAPTER 1

A dusty, blue van made its way slowly along the steep, narrow road. Its unshaven driver, the only occupant, listened to the radio and smoked frequently, the cabin strewn with spent food wrappers and discarded drink cans. It was a long familiar journey; from coastal southern Spain near the border with Gibraltar, heading inland passing by Madrid and continuing all the way through central Spain towards Zaragoza. He would cross the border into France high in the Pyrenees at a small checkpoint at El Portalet, manned by a sole border guard who he knew from experience would, for 40 Euros and a carton of cigarettes, wave the van through without checking the contents. The driver would continue heading north, through Bordeaux, en route to his ultimate destination – a small port called Carteret in Normandy.

He always travelled the deserted minor roads, avoiding the toll booths and traffic cameras of the autopistas and autovias in Spain. He would do the same in France, considerably lengthening his journey but there was no rush. He ran this route once a week and rather liked the peace and tranquillity of the minor roads. He also took advantage of the eastern European prostitutes that populated the truck stops – not something that would be tolerated at the service areas on the autopistas.

There was a particular truck stop he favoured just north of Zaragoza that was screened from the road by a line of green leafed Spanish Plane trees, their bark peeling and seeds scattered over the poorly surfaced lay-by. He had got to know a few of the girls there and he welcomed breaking the boredom of the journey. He had been married for 20 years and his wife had lost interest in sex since the children had come along.

There was a particular blonde eastern European girl, no more than 20 years old, who he had encountered on his last few trips and who he, in his mind, had named Sasha, although he had never thought to ask her name. She spoke little Spanish, just enough to understand what he wanted her to do and set a price. As he pulled off the road into the truck stop he could not see her at first. Disappointed, he wondered if she had moved on. He drove the full length of the lay-by before stopping the van and throwing a cigarette butt out of the open window.

He had parked as far away as possible from the only other vehicle in the truck stop. It was a lorry with Andorran plates and a snoozing driver, a spider's web tattoo visibly covering the whole of one cheek. As he did so he noticed in his wing mirror that Sasha was approaching the van, wearing shorts and a cropped vest. He was hard already and smiled to himself as she opened the door. She climbed across him, pressing herself against his chest and lay on the bench seat.

He was soon too absorbed to notice the rear doors of his van being opened by the tattooed driver of the Andorran lorry, who proceeded to rifle through his cargo of illegally imported, untaxed Marlboro cigarettes. The Andorran silently opened a flick knife, using it to carefully slice a two inch slit in the packaging of one of the cartons. He inserted an electronic tracking device, no larger than a credit card, before replacing the cigarette carton. He satisfied himself that there was no outward sign of interference with the van's cargo, before gently closing the rear doors and walking quickly away.

The driver's grunting climax brought on a coughing fit and, after unleashing a stream of phlegm through the still open window, he paid Sasha. He wiped himself down with a stained handkerchief, fastening his trousers as she walked away. He started the engine, noticing in the van's wing mirrors that the Andorran lorry had gone. He pulled back onto the dusty road and proceeded north.

The remaining journey would be uneventfully passed, save for the occasional smile as he recalled Sasha's firm, young body. When he reached his final destination of Carteret port on the north coast of France, he drove the van onto the quay and saw Edouard standing by his blue fishing boat. It was moored against the quay side, in the same part of the port as all of the other times. Edouard looked over and waved, placing the fishing net he was mending back into the boat. He approached the van and shook hands with the driver, exchanging pleasantries.

As they unloaded the cartons of cigarettes into the fishing boat, there was no visible sign of disruption to them from the hasty intervention that had taken place while the libidinous driver had been otherwise engaged at the truck stop.

CHAPTER 2

As I left the pontoon I looked back to check that I wasn't dragging any lines in the water and listened carefully to the engine note to check that the twin diesels were firing properly. I leant over the stern to reassure myself that the coolant water, which circulated around the engines before being expelled near the stern drives, was splashing into the wake that was being created. The water in the estuary was as calm as I had ever seen it. A spell of high pressure and the slack tide joining to ensure that the water was as flat and smooth as a lake.

The RIB's hull pierced through the glassy calm. It was around six in the morning and the sun had risen just far enough to start to put some warmth back into my hands. Salcombe was quiet onshore, but I could hear the crews of the few yachts moored on buoys in the estuary begin to stir and make the first of endless cups of tea.

The scar stretching from my chin a little way along my jaw line, throbbed slightly in the cool air. I rubbed some warmth into it with the back of my hand before zipping up the fleece lined collars of my sailing jacket over my chin. The scar was one legacy of my time in the Royal Marines, another more welcome one was my love of boating and the sea. I pulled a faded blue cap from a compartment and pulled it down tightly onto my head. My sunglasses were resting on the console and I reached for them to shield my eyes from the low-lying early morning sun.

As I reached the main channel of the estuary I pushed the throttles forward and felt the bow rise and the boat's speed begin to increase. I pushed further and the bow sank back down as the hull began to plane and then accelerate. I could hear the engines beginning to work hard and I throttled back so as not to attract too much attention. Even at this time of the morning someone would have noticed me departing if I exceeded the six-knot speed limit by too much. The engine noise receded to a quiet grumble and I enjoyed my smooth ride down the estuary towards the open sea.

I felt that familiar sense of total freedom and release from life on land as I looked out over the sand bar. I mentally plotted the course that I would take, once I had cleared that obstacle. I probably could have gone over the bar - what with the RIB unladen and the tide high - but the water was choppier there and the sand forming the bar had a habit of constantly moving and reprofiling. I fastened my lifejacket, attached the kill chord to my thigh, and steered towards the deeper channel to the west of the bar.

Meeting the open sea, I floored the throttles and got a kick from the exhilarating acceleration and the bass beat of the engines. The weather and conditions were perfect and I was going to enjoy this crossing. I was using my favourite boat - a RIB-X Rigid Inflatable Boat with bespoke twin inboard diesel engines crafted by Ilmor Racing. She was 29 feet long and capable of over 75 knots on a flat sea, and could hold 50 through pretty much anything.

The RIB-X works team had just stunned the UK offshore racing fraternity on their first attempt at the Round Britain Race with an overall second and a class win - it had serious pedigree this boat. The designer hadn't neglected form when designing her for function either - she was a fantastic looking boat with elegant but powerful lines.

The engines felt unburstable and I knew from past experience that there was no better fast boat through rough seas. Certainly nothing that the Coast Guard or Border Force had at their disposal. I leaned back against the seating post and revelled in the thrill of my fast passage. I looked back to see the coastline rapidly disappearing and marvelled at the sun glistening in the rooster tail of water being thrown up by the twin sterndrives. It was going to be a gorgeous day and the crossing was going to be fun. This was payback for the cold, wet and thoroughly miserable weekly trips that I had made throughout the winter.

I set my GPS navigation unit to La Fontenelle on the North East tip of Guernsey in the Channel Islands. I was intending to then head clockwise around the eastern coastline to St Peter Port, where I could refuel and grab some breakfast, before heading on closer towards the French coastline. The sea was picking up slightly, so I throttled back a little and trimmed the bow down to cleave through the swell. I was alone at sea with no other vessels immediately visible and I enjoyed the solitude and anticipation that was so familiar to me from undertaking this crossing so many times before. The only company for me were a few gulls wheeling overhead and, from time to time, the odd cargo ship pummelling up and down the shipping lane that ran from east to west along the Channel Sea.

Concentrating hard on reading the sea conditions and monitoring my course, time flew by. Any off-shore trip, no matter how calm the conditions, requires vigilance and respect. I could soon pick out the rocky headland of Guernsey's shore. As I got closer I could see a fishing boat on its way back from an overnight trip, accompanied by a cloud of gulls no doubt after the surplus catch that would be thrown overboard so as not to exceed some arbitrary quota imposed by a bureaucrat in an office wholly removed from the sea.

I slowed as I reached the rougher water caused by the tide and currents racing round the island. The RIB could easily have powered through the chop but I didn't want the attention that might come from such a spectacle and my legs were already tired from absorbing the pounding of the two hour crossing. I soon picked up the forest of masts that heralded my arrival at the marina in St Peter Port and headed to the refuelling pontoon where a sleepy attendant threw me some mooring lines.

"Where have you come from this morning then?" I ignored his question, feigning to have missed it, and busied myself with the proffered fuel line.

"Could you fill her right up while I find some breakfast?" I asked as I climbed onto the pontoon and headed to a café I knew along the dockside. I had a couple of hours to kill before needing to head off again and had a hunger for a cigarette and a café au lait in the sunshine, warming me through after the wind-chill from the crossing. While waiting for my coffee I called Vilda on my mobile and asked her to check with Edouard that we were still OK to rendezvous at 10 am.

...

Sitting at the table behind Luttrell, the man ostensibly reading a tourist brochure while enjoying a coffee, wrote the names "Vilda" and "Edouard" into a small notebook concealed within the brochure. He was very overweight, his new yellow polo shirt stretched over but not quite concealing his round, protruding stomach. His balding head was sunburnt bright red and peeling, sweat beading on his forehead. Tufts of chest hair sprouting from the open neck of his shirt. He wiped his brow with a handkerchief as he made a note of the time that Luttrell arrived at the café and the exact contents of the brief conversation, so far as he had been able to overhear them. He also wrote a detailed description of Luttrell's appearance:

180 cm tall. Athletic build. Short brown hair, lightened by the sun. Tanned and weather beaten complexion. Blue eyes. Military bearing. Prominent scar from chin along right hand jaw line. Grey Musto sailing jacket and faded brown trousers with cargo pockets. Sebago sailing shoes.

He had been on Guernsey watching out for Luttrell

for nearly a week now, each evening so far filing a report that simply stated "No show". This evening's report would be different and he needed to ensure that every detail was correct.

CHAPTER 3

I sipped my café au lait and watched St Peter Port start to wake up. There were few fishing boats moored here anymore, replaced by shiny, white Sunseekers and Fairlines, fully crewed and spotlessly maintained but rarely ever used. I had been making this trip once a week for the last three years and St Peter Port, the whole of Guernsey in fact, still left me cold. It was beautiful, stunningly located and affluent but its population of bankers and money men gave it all the character of a trophy wife. Its natural beauty should have made me never want to leave, but I couldn't have lived there for a week.

I know that Vilda felt the same way. I could see it in her downcast face as she walked along the quay towards the café, not yet realising that I was sitting watching her. She had been staying here for those three years in an apartment that I rented just back from the waterfront.

To the outside world, I was a former Royal Marine turned successful boat dealer based in Salcombe, Devon specialising in shafting the city dwellers who descended en masse on Salcombe during their children's school holidays and who thought nothing of spending their excessive bonuses on overpowered Boston Whalers and RIBs. For the most part, they were only used to ferry their families back and forth to the beaches in the estuary – the wilder ones occasionally even breaking the six knot speed limit.

The boatyard, though, was the perfect base from which I could make my trips across the Channel to pick up contraband cigarettes with no tax or duty paid and smuggle them back to the UK. I bought them for a quarter of their retail price in the UK and their size, weight and waterproof packaging made them ideal for bringing in by boat. My frequent trips on the RIB-X or my yacht wouldn't raise an eyebrow locally, particularly as I let it be known that I was seeing a girl living on Guernsey.

I had two staff at the yard and they looked after it, more or less, whenever I was away. In an affluent place like Salcombe, the boats pretty much sold themselves. Everyone wanted to buy into the lifestyle. I kept a 40 foot Najad yacht on a mooring in the estuary and if the weather would have made a crossing in the RIB unpleasant, I just used that instead. It made for a slower trip, but offered better shelter from the elements and saved a small fortune in fuel.

"Hi!" Vilda sat in my lap and looked into my face with her big blue eyes. She was a Swede I had met when backpacking around Thailand after I was kicked out of the Marines and we had ended up travelling together - diving, partying and having sex, at every available opportunity. I knew the look on her face. She was dying of boredom out here but, bizarrely, that boredom and loneliness seemed to have the same effect on her as the strong weed we used to smoke while drinking the favourite backpacker cocktail of Thai whisky, Coca Cola and crushed amphetamine "diet" pills. Two joints and a couple of glasses of that potent brew, watch her pupils dilate and her body come alive.

I kissed her hard on the lips, my free hand gripping one firm buttock. "Let's go to the boat. We are not meeting Edouard for a couple of hours and we can take it somewhere a little more private!" I placed my hand on her waist and walked with her down to the boat. I paid for the fuel and then started the engines while Vilda released the mooring lines and pushed us off the pontoon.

As soon as we were out of the port I pulled her body hard against mine, looking out for oncoming traffic over her shoulder. I was leaning back against the helm seat and she stood with her legs either side of my right thigh and her hand on my crotch. It would take fifteen minutes to reach the rendez-vous point with Edouard - Dixcart Bay on the south side of the neighbouring island, Sark, and we would have to wait. I rammed the throttles open and the twin engines roared as the RIB pounded through the waves. As we passed the headland to the Bay, I was pleased to see that there were no other boats there and I throttled back until we were just drifting. We fell on each other, light headed and panting with desire. It was urgent, frantic even. Our bodies desperately and instinctively making up for the week that we had just spent apart.

I lit a cigarette. "I'm just gonna bring us in closer to the shore and drop the anchor. Edouard is due in an hour or so and I fancy a swim." The water was crystal clear and as we got closer to the beach I could easily see the bottom. When we were in a couple of metres of water I let the anchor go together with a few lengths of anchor chain, watching it bite into the sand as the boat's momentum pulled the anchor line tight. Vilda was already in the water:

"That feels so good, can you bring the masks with you?" I briefly sat on the inflated tubes while I adjusted my mask then slipped off into the water, letting myself go right under for a couple of seconds. It was cold but it was very refreshing to feel the warm sun on my face while the water cooled my body.

"Here, take your mask, shall we snorkel out to those rocks and take a look around?" I trod water as I placed my mask against my face and pulled the strap back over my head. Vilda set off fast, swimming crawl, but I grabbed her ankle and roughly pulled her back to me. I held her naked body against mine, taking the snorkel out of the way and kissing her full on her cool, fresh mouth.

"Has everything been OK this past week?" She shook her head. "No, I've been bored to hell and missing you." "Well I'm here now and the way things are going we won't have to keep doing this for too much longer." I kissed her, more gently this time, then we swam in a fast crawl heading out to a group of rocks that just broke the surface, halfway to the beach.

I wanted to really swim and Vilda was with me stroke for stroke. As we approached the rocks we swam over a small octopus sheltering in some weed at the foot of the rocks. It got spooked and soon disappeared into a nearby crevice and we made for the beach, lying on the sand and letting the sun warm and dry us off. We had the place to ourselves and we made love again on the beach, this time at a slower, gentler pace. Her body tanned and glistening in the late morning light.

"Edouard is going to be here in ten minutes. I am going to swim back to the boat and get ready for the handover." Vilda rolled off my back, she had been lying on me while I dozed on my front on the sandy beach. The cool water invigorated me and I quickly covered the 200 metres to the boat, Vilda right behind me. I pulled myself up and over the inflatable tubes near the stern and then lowered the short bathing ladder for Vilda. I reached for my binoculars from the cubby under the helm and surveyed the bay.

"Not a soul about. Shame, they would have enjoyed watching us on the beach!"

I turned and looked over to mainland France, some twenty miles to the east. I couldn't see the land itself but could see several fishing boats plying the coastal waters, one was heading in our direction. As she drew closer I recognised the blue hull and red superstructure of Edouard's fishing boat.

I prepared two lines to secure the RIB to his boat when he pulled alongside. He seemed to be motoring against the current or the tide and was making slow progress. We were sheltered in the bay, but I figured that he was probably also heading straight into the wind. I looked around again to check that the handover wouldn't be observed, but could see only a few fishing boats, lying much closer to the French coast.

I motored over to the headland at the end of the

bay and looked towards Guernsey to check on the conditions for our short return journey. I was surprised to see a UK Border Force patrol boat making its way up the narrow channel between the islands. Its' white paintwork glinting in the sun. They didn't regularly patrol this far south and I guessed that it had circum-navigated Guernsey as part of an exercise and would then continue back across the Channel.

We had been hidden from it in the bay and I was unconcerned – if they had spotted us they would have just taken us for a couple out on a day trip, intending to swim and picnic in the bay. I watched the patrol boat continue north along the channel between Sark and Guernsey and was relieved to see it maintain its course until it was nearly out of sight. It always surprised me how fast those large boats could travel. I turned to see that Edouard was approaching the bay from the other end and accelerated over to him, the sudden turn of speed raising a shout from Vilda as she was forced to hang on.

Edouard's boat was motionless when we reached him and I brought the RIB along the seaward side of him where we wouldn't be visible to anyone on the shore. "Bonjour Edouard, tout va bien?" He answered in heavily accented English "The weather, it makes good today and I will catch plenty, here take this, prends". Vilda caught the thrown line and tied us off to his boat as Edouard started to hand me the cartons of cigarettes. Each carton held 200 cigarettes, ten packets of 20, and I always took 200 cartons. It was enough to make the trip worthwhile, but still easily stowed out of sight in the various lockers on the RIB. Once Vilda and I had got them all secured, I took a waterproof bag of euro notes from the bottom of the anchor locker.

I paid Edouard a sum equal to 25% of the UK retail price of the cigarettes. I didn't concern myself with what he paid his supplier or where he got them from - that was his business. He once mentioned that they were driven up from Spain, presumably originating in North Africa and shipped over, but I didn't care or want to know. Disposing of them in the UK would make me a profit of around ten grand each trip and I had been making this trip pretty much once a week for the last three years.

It was easy money, a little exciting, and I felt no guilt whatsoever for depriving the tax man in the United Kingdom. Was I really doing anything different to the thousands of weekly booze-cruisers returning from France with a sunburnt face and overladen with cheap booze?

"OK Edouard, merci, I will see you at the same time next week. If anything changes, Vilda will let you know". I rarely spoke directly with him, other than face to face when picking up a shipment. He and Vilda had each other's mobile numbers and would speak if arrangements needed to change due to weather or unforeseen circumstances, but the less contact the better. We left Edouard to his fishing and cruised back to St Peter Port and lunch in the sun on the quayside.

I stayed with Vilda in the apartment that night, leaving the boat on a secure pontoon in the marina.

She talked constantly, glad of the company, and we discussed our plans. I figured we had a couple more months of these weekly trips before we had made enough to move on to what we both wanted next – a quiet finca in Mallorca, not too far from the coast and where we could be together. I would build up a boat sales business and get my kicks taking tourists on fast RIB rides, maybe start a diving school. Perhaps a couple of blonde headed children would come along and change our lives, for the better, permanently.

We woke early the next morning, still wrapped in each other's arms. I checked the weather forecast on my iPhone – the conditions were going to be fine for my passage back to the mainland, with a light wind, only a small swell expected and little chance of rain. We breakfasted on strong coffee and a croissant at a café, before we said our goodbyes and I returned to the boat. It was only 7 am and the marina was silent, the start-up of the twin diesel engines briefly shattering the peace until the engines settled to a lumpy idle. As I cast off I noticed a ship moving beyond the mouth of the marina. It was the same UK Border Force patrol boat that I had seen yesterday. It was heading in the opposite direction to me and I didn't give it another thought as I manoeuvred away from the pontoon and headed out to sea.

I wrapped the kill-cord around my thigh, zipped up my yachting jacket and opened the throttles. The big RIB instantly surged onto the plane and accelerated forward until I eased off to a fast cruise of 30 or so knots - the 70 mile passage back to Salcombe would only take a couple of hours at most. Once properly off-shore (and away from any tut-tutting and fist waving yachties) I could push the boat harder and revel in her off-shore performance. The way she beat wave-chop into submission was like watching a steam roller flattening a molehill. In rough weather you could literally jump her from wave crest to wave crest, the engine revs ascending and descending as the propellers briefly spun freely in the air before submerging once again in the next wave.

The crossing was uneventful, but exhilarating, and I was almost disappointed to see the outline of Bolt Head coming into view. I was soon over the sand bar at the mouth of the estuary - the tide was in - and the 6 knot limit up the estuary felt deathly slow after the fast passage. I used the time to make the boat look like it had just been used for a leisure trip, draping towels and water sports gear over the seats and on the deck. The contraband was safely hidden out of sight in the boat's lockers and my wet suit and diving gear, visibly scattered over the deck, would satisfy the curiosity of any onlooker.

I brought the RIB alongside the floating pontoon at my boatyard and opened up the storefront. Business as usual. Salcombe is a busy little town, even out of season, and I waited until nightfall before recovering the cigarettes from the RIB and loading them straight into the boot of my Audi, safely parked in one of the boatyard's old buildings - away from prying eyes.

CHAPTER 4

The Audi was a red RS6 Avant with a 4.0 litre twin-turbo V8 engine. A joy to drive, with supercar levels of performance, but enough space in the boot to hold the consignment of cigarettes. Not the most discrete way to travel, but not exactly out of place, either, in upmarket Salcombe where the second home owners, mostly Londoners engaged in who knows what financial chicanery, liked to come and go in some pretty exotic machinery. I didn't need the Sat Nav - I had made this trip hundreds of times before - and as the sun came up headed north to Hereford listening to a few favourite tunes from my iPod.

It was a road trip of 175 miles, mostly motorway, but with some fantastic driving roads once I had crossed over the Severn Bridge into Wales. The road following the Wye Valley as it meandered up to Hereford. My cousin, Sean, ran a business selling crop and grass seed to farmers and agribusinesses and his products were distributed to his customers by a team of trusted lorry drivers that he had gathered together over time. They would pick up the pallets of seeds from his warehouse and deliver them to his customers nationwide. They would also, for cash in hand, deliver the cigarettes to wholesale businesses and middlemen in the West Midlands, before in turn being sold in pubs, clubs, corner stores and anywhere else that the smokers wouldn't question the non-UK packaging and doubtful provenance.

The trip through Devon and Somerset was uneventful and I reached the old Severn Bridge, near Bristol, to cross over into Wales in seemingly no time at all. As I decelerated for the toll booth, I noticed a grey BMW 5 series pulling up at the neighbouring booth with two thick-necked, sunglass wearing occupants in the front seat. Mirrored lenses reflected the lights of the toll booth. In such a fast car as the Audi, I was always on the look-out for unmarked Police cars but was reassured to see that these guys were not wearing uniforms, albeit that they did seem to be staring straight at the Audi. Who could blame them, any car lover would?

Just to make absolutely sure, I purposefully fumbled with my change and let them pull away first. I kept my speed down and followed them along the motorway until I turned off, without indicating, up towards Chepstow and then the fantastic driving road running alongside the River Wye. It was always traffic free and the scenery was stunning as it hugged the wooded valley floor all the way up to Monmouth. I was maintaining a sensible pace but not "on it" as I was at the same time trying to do the mental maths to calculate what this shipment would earn me and who would need to be paid what.

I slowed for the red traffic light at a narrow bridge that crosses over the river. I casually glanced in the rear view mirror and was startled to notice that the same grey 5 Series from earlier was closing up on me from behind. I had watched them drive straight past the turning for the motorway junction for this road. They must have really flown to have come off at a later junction, circled back, made up the ground and caught up with me. Why? How had they known my route? I could have taken any of several roads after coming off that motorway junction. It couldn't be just a coincidence.

I purposefully stalled the Audi when the traffic light turned green, waited for the red stop-light, and then powered across the bridge, looking in the rear view mirror to see what they would do. They followed straight through the red light, headlights flashing away a warning to the oncoming traffic. I stamped the accelerator into the carpet and gunned the big Audi as fast as it would go. The noise from the V8 would have woken the dead as I revved it to the redline. As the V8 bass beat morphed into a feral yowl, it was like being picked up by the scruff of the neck and thrown down the road. It was always astonishing just how much grip the four wheel drive generated on greasy, leaf strewn corners before catapulting the car along the straights. I knew this road well and I had soon opened up a sizeable gap.

As the road twisted and turned, I was soon out of sight of the following car and dived into a side turning and quickly parked in a gateway, killing the driving lights and ignition. I wound down the window and heard them drive past. I waited until I could no longer hear their engine note before I reversed back on to the main road and headed back the way I had come.

I retraced my steps but as I approached the bridge from the opposite direction I saw the grey BMW in my rear view mirror and it was heading back towards me, travelling fast. They must have some sort of tracking device to have so quickly realised their error and I struggled to think - the Audi had been securely parked in a storeroom at the boatyard and so I was sure there was nothing on the car itself, it must be in the cargo of cigarettes!

I ignored the traffic lights and quickly crossed the bridge just in front of a tractor coming the other way, fortunately blocking the bridge while it slowly crossed. Its trailer just slightly narrower than the width of the bridge itself. I flipped the electronic tailgate, jumped out of the car and jettisoned the cigarettes onto the roadside. I tore off up the road with the tailgate closing warning still beeping in my ear - I hadn't waited for it to close. The tractor had cleared the bridge and I could see in my rear view mirror that the BMW was now accelerating hard back across the bridge.

Driving fast and determinedly, with adrenalin pounding through my veins and heightening my senses, I soon lost them. As the road passed through a woodland I turned off the main road and took a poorly surfaced track, until I was hidden from view. I parked up, hurriedly disconnected my phone, and ran for cover in the trees. I waited, literally holding my breath, but the BMW travelled straight past me. I heard its engine being worked hard as it powered along the valley road.

I gave it a couple more minutes before returning to the Audi and retraced my steps to the abandoned cigarettes on the roadside. I tore the packaging open and found a credit card sized, black electronic device, warm to the touch. I stamped on it, breaking it open to reveal the circuitry inside before throwing it into the river. I quickly reloaded the cargo, throwing it into the boot, and drove off up the road continuing my journey. I took an alternative route as soon as I could. I looked out for it constantly but didn't see the grey BMW again.

It was around a forty minute drive to my cousin's warehouse and I constantly checked to see if I was being followed. Nothing. I took one more detour just before arriving at the warehouse and parked up waiting, but I was in the clear and so drove on to the warehouse. I parked the Audi inside and quickly closed the shutter doors to ensure that it could not be seen from the road. My mind was racing but I said nothing to Sean, who was using his forklift to store a new delivery of agricultural seed. I waved and unloaded the cigarettes while listening out for the tell-tale crunch of tyres in the yard outside - nothing.

After half an hour or so I felt that I could relax a little and I spent the rest of the day helping Sean store the large shipment of crop seed. It was thirsty work and Sean asked if I would like to stay over and have a night out in Hereford. My mind had been feverishly considering who might have followed me and why? I was glad to spend the night there and leave the car undercover, letting the trail go cold while I considered my next move.

The tracking device must have been placed in the cigarette packaging before Edouard delivered the shipment to me - the cigarettes had gone straight into lockable storage lockers on the boat and from there into my car. I thought back and was sure that the lockers hadn't shown any signs of having been tampered with when I returned to the boat in the marina at St Peter Port after my night on Guernsey with Vilda. I had some thinking to do.

Sean and I went to a pub we knew well, the Spread Eagle in the centre of Hereford. An old black and white, timbered building with a dark, gloomy interior. A good place for a few beers and to catch up with Sean without being overheard. That night, it was the usual mixture of students, farm boys on the lash and local girls hoping to pick up a demi-god from the Regiment, looking for the thrill of being with a Special Forces soldier. Besides housing the HQ for the SAS, there wasn't a great deal else that Hereford nightlife had to offer, so who could blame them?

Watching the girls' predatory antics in the bar with a couple of deeply suntanned guys who had clearly just returned from an overseas mission entertained us for a while, but I couldn't stop running the events of the day over and over in my head. I said nothing about what had happened to Sean. I wanted hard facts before I set any hares running.

CHAPTER 5

I headed off early the next day and drove back down south to Salcombe, constantly monitoring the vehicles around me for anything unusual. The journey was uneventful and the miles passed quickly by, but it did give me time to think. The only authorities possibly interested in my smuggling activities would be the UK Border Force. They were tasked with managing border control for the United Kingdom and enforcing immigration and customs regulations. They were woefully under resourced and I couldn't believe that such a small operation as mine would have come to their attention.

Nonetheless, my mind kept returning to the UK Border Force vessel that I had seen on two occasions when picking up the last shipment - it couldn't be just a coincidence and I decided that they must have been tracking the shipment even then.

As I approached Salcombe, I pulled the car over in a quiet lane and checked over every inch of the car, inside and out. There was nothing visibly untoward and I felt confident that I was no longer being tracked. The car had been stored securely in the boatyard storeroom while I was in Guernsey and the problems so far only related to this latest shipment.

I returned to the boatyard and resumed the, hopefully, innocent façade of a boatyard owner. I spoke to Vilda on her mobile, listening intently to what she was saying to see if she had noticed anything unusual. I didn't want to discuss what had happened on the phone - the paranoia of the persecuted had set in - but I did want to sound her out and warn her to be vigilant. There was no news, other than that she was bored in Guernsey and desperate to leave - which was hardly news. With just a few further shipments planned, I reasoned with her to be patient and see it through.

The next rendezvous with Edouard was only four days away and there was no choice but to sit tight and see what transpired. Time passes slowly when you expect an imminent knock on the door, but nothing happened and I was relieved when the day came to make the trip. I set off earlier than usual - an hour or so before it got light on the day before we were due to rendezvous with Edouard. The weather forecast was for patchy rain, low visibility and a fairly rough sea.

It was nothing that the RIB-X couldn't easily cope with and at least the poor visibility would prevent anyone from tracking the boat by sight. I had already checked her over prior to departure, even hauling her out to check the underside of the hull, but she was clean of any tracking device. I was working on the assumption that any further attempt to track me would be made in the same way as before - hidden in the cargo rather than in or on the boat itself. I set the GPS for St Peter Port and fought my way through the wind and rain.

The crossing was hard work and miserable but uneventful and, fortunately, the rain showers had passed by the time I reached Guernsey. I arrived in bright sunshine. I had asked Vilda to meet me in the marina and we played up the role of lovers who had been apart for a week. It wasn't hard, she met the boat in shorts and a bikini top, bare-footed. Her figure was too good for her not to attract attention but, hey, she lived there, the locals knew her and what was the point of hiding away? She was my cover story and was all the justification anyone would ever need for a sea crossing in rough weather!

I grabbed my bag and we made our way along the quay to her apartment. I had planned to sit down and talk her through what had happened, but being apart for a week inevitably meant we made straight for the bedroom. It smelt of marijuana and I could tell from Vilda's dilated pupils that she had been smoking a few joints. Not only did it make her totally uninhibited, but it seemed to heighten her sensitivity. We pulled off each other's clothes and stood body to body, skin to skin, kissing passionately. My body responded to hers and the room breathed with our excitement. There is no more powerful aphrodisiac than feeling and hearing the woman you love building to a crescendo, stalling and teasing her until we were both spent.

I pulled the covers partially over us and shared a cigarette. Her long, blonde hair falling between her breasts as we lay facing each other, our limbs still entwined.

"Has everything been OK this week, angel?" One of her breasts still cupped by my hand, feeling her heart beating strongly.

"Yea, it's been fine. I have been studying and had three shifts in the bar since I saw you last".

I looked intently into her eyes. "I think I was followed when I delivered the last shipment of cigarettes to the warehouse in Hereford. Two men in a BMW followed me for a couple of miles and I tried to lose them at a stoplight, but they just drove through even though it was on red. I managed to lose them but they reappeared later on and I found what I think was a tracking device in one of the cartons of cigarettes. I managed to throw the tracker in a river and got away from them." She sat up, looking shocked.

I asked: "Are you sure that everything has been normal this week?"

She paused and thought, her even features scrunched in concern, and then said "While I was working in the bar one evening I got chatted up by a guy who was drinking in the bar by himself. He wouldn't leave me alone. He wasn't from the island and said that he was a lawyer over here for business. He did look like a lawyer - fat and bald - but I thought that it was strange that he would be by himself if he was on a business trip? He asked me a lot of questions and was very persistent".

I made her repeat their entire conversation, word for word as far as she could remember, but it could just have been totally innocent and unconnected. As for her being chatted up, well, don't date a stunning blonde who works in a bar and expect her not to get attention! That didn't bother me, but we were going to have to be really cautious when we picked up the next shipment from Edouard tomorrow.

I told her not to worry, that it was just a one off, and that they hadn't managed to follow me all of the way to the warehouse or successfully intercept the shipment. We were in the clear.

Mollified slightly, Vilda jumped out of bed and padded over to the bathroom to run a bath. She called from the bathroom, raising her voice above the running water:

"Do you fancy eating at Mora tonight?" Vilda worked in the basement bar at Mora - atmospheric lighting, a vaulted barrel-like ceiling and an underground feel. On the floor above there is a restaurant with good food that overlooked the marina.

"Yes, sure. Let's have a cocktail in the bar to kick off with?" I lit a cigarette and thought about tomorrow's pick-up. I planned to get there early, watch Edouard's approach carefully, and if there was the slightest hint of anything unusual we could bug out and hot foot it back to Salcombe - nothing would live with the RIB-X on that crossing, if it had to be used in anger.

Vilda emerged from the bathroom, pink cheeked, and I jumped into her bath. I soaked a while then shaved, standing in the bath so that I could see the mirror. She had bitten me on the chest and I could still see the teeth marks around my nipple. I smiled to myself as I imagined payback for that particular little display of affection. As I came out of the bathroom, Vilda was already dressed and drying her hair. She looked hot in a little black dress - all glowing caramel tanned skin and silky long legs.

We walked hand in hand along the cobbled streets of the port, bathed in the warm glow of the sunset. I held the door as she went first into the bar area. Despite the gloom, heads were turning her way as we walked up to the bar. I caught up with her colleagues and friends and ordered the cocktails - a Black Crush for Vilda, while I rebooted with a Coffee Caipirinha. It was strong and powerful, refreshing after the joint that we had just shared on the way up to the bar. I was picking up on Vilda's mood - she clearly wanted to enjoy her night off, and I smiled inwardly at the thought of the night to come.

They didn't have a table free upstairs for another couple of hours and so we each chose the next cocktail for the other, a Black Sunrise for me and I picked a raspberry and peach Bellini for Vilda - which she requested had a shot of vodka in too. It was getting crowded at the bar and we pressed together, shouting into each other's ear. The Bellini was ice cold, the pureed raspberry and peach had obviously been chilling for some time and her glass was thoroughly frosted.

I had a couple of the buttons on my shirt undone and Vilda kept pressing the glass against the indent where my throat joined my chest. She laughed as the odd bead of condensation ran down my chest. It was a real contrast to have an ice cold glass pressed against my skin in a hot, crowded bar and I thought back to my earlier resolve for payback - the nipple felt bruised. I pinched her ass deliberately and, as she let out a yelp, walked straight out to the smoking terrace.

There was nobody else out there and I pulled a joint out of my shirt pocket and lit up, inhaling long and deep. As I exhaled I felt Vilda's arm reach around me from behind and pull my chin round to face her. She took the joint and finished it while I ran my fingernails up her bare thigh. I kissed her hard and manoeuvred her against a wall in the dark, my legs between hers. I pushed her short skirt further up and she unbuckled my belt. It was frantic and rough, the danger of being interrupted somehow adding to the excitement.

We both lit up afterwards and as I held her firmly, whispered: "You could drive any man mad, do you know that? I can't imagine ever being bored by you."

She kissed me and said: "How much longer should we keep smuggling? Why don't we forget tomorrow's pick-up and just clear out? We have saved enough now and let's not take the risk. I am worried about you having been followed - it can only mean that we have been found out, no?"

I thought for a while and said; "We are here now and we can be careful tomorrow. Let's do this one last run. We can use this trip to pay off Sean and the distribution guys. Why don't you pack tonight and we can take everything in the boat in the morning? It seems crazy to have brought the boat all the way over here and confirmed the rendezvous with Edouard, only to not go through with it. Let's do this one last consignment and we can then just walk away from Guernsey and smuggling for good." She nodded.

We walked back inside the bar and made our way to the table upstairs. As we eat, we planned what we would do in Mallorca and the next stage in our life together. We shared a bottle of white Rioja to celebrate our Iberian future.

CHAPTER 6

The plans for an early start had been hijacked by last night's hedonism and I opened my eyes to a blinding headache, a mental fog. I looked at my phone, it was already 7.30 and we were due to meet Edouard at ten. I pulled the duvet off Vilda and pinched her toe until she came around. "Wake up sleeping beauty, it's late and you need to pack your stuff." She groaned and tried to fight to pull the covers back. I will never understand why a hangover makes me feel horny, but I resisted the temptation to jump back into bed with her and went to make coffee.

I helped Vilda pack her things and we stumbled around the apartment, groaning and grumbling at each other, while the possessions collected over the last three years of her life were hurriedly considered then packed or abandoned. It took several trips to take her holdalls and suitcase to the boat. She posted the keys through the letting agent's door and we grabbed a croissant and some bottled water as we hurriedly returned to the marina.

It was a clear day, with just a light breeze and the sun was already beginning to cast its warmth. I still felt cold and hung over and Vilda evidently felt the same, hunched against the stern seat and monosyllabic in that peculiarly Scandinavian way. We were due to meet Edouard at the usual rendezvous on Sark in 15 minutes and that would leave no time to scout out and observe the bay, as I had planned. I felt sick to the stomach and it wasn't just the hangover.

. . .

The fat, balding man who had noted Luttrell's arrival the previous week, stood outside of the apartment building and observed, unseen, as the last bags were carried out of the apartment. He watched Luttrell and Vilda head along the quay to the marina. He waited for a few minutes to ensure that they would not return, before entering into the lobby floor of the apartment building. He walked slowly and silently up the stairs to the front door of the abandoned apartment. He paused, holding his breath, his eyes darting from side to side. Satisfied, he slipped on a pair of surgical gloves before pushing a lozenge shaped metal implement into the door jamb until, with a click, the lock slid back and the door opened.

He walked into the apartment, carefully pushing the door closed behind him. He began his work. From the leather holdall that he was carrying he took two paper packets containing a white and brown powder and shook out the contents – one over the kitchen counter and the other over the shelving in the bathroom. He took out several sheets of typed paper and placed them under the bed. He picked up his bag and gently pulled the front door closed behind him. He removed the gloves, placing them in the bag, before descending the stairs into the lobby and walking out into the street.

...

The twin diesels started on the first turn and I waited for the lumpy engine note to settle to a deep, throbbing idle before casting off the shore lines. I powered through the marina at three times the speed limit before gunning the throttles, navigating by sight for nearby Sark. The passage was fast, running before the prevailing wind. We shortly rounded the headland and Dixcart Bay came into view.

The only boat visible in the vicinity was Edouard's blue and red fishing boat, anchored in the deepest part of the bay. I turned towards him and the big RIB heeled, carving a turn, while I throttled back, shouting to Vilda "I can't see anyone else here and everything looks fine. I'll deal with Edouard, you just stay vigilant and keep an eye out for any other boats, OK?" A sullen nod, in reply.

We came alongside Edouard's boat and I attached two lines, holding the RIB's tubing against the wooden hull of his boat. He was alone. "Ca va Edouard, qu'est-ce qui se passe?" "Not like you to be late Simon, had something better to do?" He winked, jerking his chin towards Vilda.

"How was your crossing? Anything unusual?" My French wasn't up to catching his full reply but it seemed to be along the lines of "the sea doesn't have a usual, it lives and breathes". I smiled and relaxed, nothing looked out of place and I could see the cargo of cigarettes just inside the little wheelhouse. We made the exchange and I released the mooring lines and left him to go off and fish. I had decided that I didn't want to tell Edouard that this would be the last consignment – I wanted no-one to know of our plans.

I smiled at Vilda "OK my angel, I think we can relax. Let's open up the shipment and just check that there is nothing hidden this time." Evidently, she was still suffering with a hangover because I didn't get an answer but she did, slowly, move from the bench seat, first putting on some music through the iPod connection at the helm. She turned the volume right up, before joining me on the foredeck. I cut into the bale of plastic wrapping to reveal the cigarette cartons inside.

Each carton was cellophane wrapped in the tobacco manufacturer's wrapping, which acted as a tamperproof seal. Nevertheless, we shook and figured the weight of each one to see if anything other than cigarettes was inside. It took some time but I let the boat drift, the tide moving us slowly away from the beach and into deeper water. We checked and re-checked the cigarettes, both of us kneeling on the deck of the boat protected by the high level of the tubes, but could find nothing untoward.

Suddenly, I felt the boat jolt and jumped to my feet. In that split second my mind feverishly searched for the cause. Had I miscalculated the tide and we had run aground? As my head rose above the RIB's tubes I could see that we were further out from the land and I whirled round, hearing Vilda loudly exhale as I did so.

Hard against the starboard bow was another vessel, military grey and slightly larger than the RIB. There were four uniformed crew, three of whom were securing the boats together while the fourth addressed us: "Good morning, I am Immigration Officer Dickinson of the UK Border Force. We have reason to believe that this vessel is involved in the fraudulent evasion of excise duty. Please identify yourselves and confirm your vessel's name." I hadn't heard them approach us, over the music playing. Cigarette cartons were strewn all over the deck of the RIB, we weren't in good shape.

"I'm Simon Luttrell and the vessel's name is Quicksilver. What can we help you with officer?" I had decided to try to brazen it out.

"And you miss, your name?" "Vilda Neilsen. What is this all about?"

He moved towards us, leaning over the hull of his vessel. "Simon Luttrell and Vilda Neilsen, we are arresting you, and impounding your vessel. We have reasonable grounds to suspect you to be committing, have committed or be guilty of an indictable offence, namely the fraudulent evasion of excise duty being a breach of either or both of the Customs & Excise Management Act 1979 and the Proceeds of Crime Act 2002. You do not have to say anything, but it may harm your defence if you do not mention when questioned something which you later rely on in court. Anything you do say may be given in evidence."

I looked at the cigarette cartons strewn around our feet and shrugged, so be it. I manoeuvred Vilda to sit next to me on the port tube breathing in her ear not to worry, while they secured Quicksilver with a line from her bow to a stern cleat on their vessel. The crew ushered us aboard their boat, while Officer Dickinson radioed ahead. We motored forward and as we rounded the headland I saw their mother ship riding at anchor in the channel between Guernsey and Sark. It was the same vessel that I had noticed last week.

I was sat next to Vilda and hurriedly whispered: "Don't worry Angel, cigarette smuggling is such a minor offence, we'll get a slap on the wrists and a paltry fine at worst. They will probably interview us under caution and take photos of the cigarette cartons, before confiscating them. Request a solicitor before they interview you and ask to be represented by the same solicitor that I will use. There will be some dumb-ass duty brief that will get called. It will be rough for 24 hours or so but don't worry, stay strong. Stick to the cover story, you know, I'm a boat dealer, you work in a bar, we met travelling and tell them the truth - you won't trip up that way - but when they get to asking about the smuggling, just say "no comment" to everything. Until we hear what they have got against us, let's not give them any information to work with. For all they can prove, this is our only trip". She nodded and I leant into her, kissing her cheek. We embarked onto the larger Border Force ship and I gave her hand a squeeze before they led us away to separate cabins.

The cabin was sparse - just a chair, table and an empty locker. No porthole and the size of the ship meant that it was difficult to tell if we were moving or not. After twenty minutes there was a knock on the door and I was offered a hot drink. I sipped my tea and asked where we were headed.

"You are being transported to Portsmouth for questioning by a detective from HM Customs & Excise, who are our partnering agency in this type of prosecution. If you need to use the conveniences let me know, otherwise, sit tight and we expect to be in Portsmouth in a couple of hours." He smirked. "I don't suppose you will be needing a cigarette will you?" He closed the cabin door and I was left to study the grey paintwork of the inside of the cabin for the rest of the trip.

We arrived at Portsmouth and were escorted to the Border Force offices there. An ugly 60s concrete block monstrosity, where a custody sergeant took my details and recorded and retained everything that was in my pockets. I asked for a solicitor and they seemed surprised that I didn't have a retained "brief", just waiting for me to call. The custody sergeant said that they would request the duty solicitor to attend me. I didn't see Vilda as I was taken to a small, dingy room euphemistically called a "holding suite". I was in the claustrophobic cell for a couple of hours and managed to briefly doze off a couple of times before the solicitor arrived.

He looked like he was wearing someone else's suit and my guess was that the previous owner wouldn't be coming back to reclaim it anytime soon. The jacket hung off his rounded shoulders and the trousers rested in folds on top of his shoes. He placed a battered briefcase on the floor and introduced himself as Mr

Gardner, without giving a first name, and ran through the details that the custody sergeant had given him.

He explained in a dull monotone that any discussions he and I would have would be legally privileged. He stressed that he couldn't attend the interview with me knowing what I was saying was a lie and therefore to first consider carefully what I said to him. I told him who I was and a brief rundown of what had happened when the Border Force guys intercepted us. Nothing more. I wanted to hear what evidence they had before responding meaningfully to their questions. He nodded and we agreed that I would provide them with my personal details at interview, but reply "no comment" to everything else.

I was placed in an interview room containing a table, four chairs and a recording machine. My solicitor and I sat on one side of the table and waited. I expected the interview to be a farce, Officer Dickinson and the guy from HM Revenue & Customs asking me the same questions over and over again with me replying "no comment" each time. It continued that way for an hour or so and it became increasingly hard to keep repeating the "no comment" mantra, so I switched tack asking them why they hadn't disclosed any evidence - witness statements, photos, anything - to us before the interview began?

I figured that they would have to either charge us for the one trip they had interrupted or, if they knew of the earlier trips, bail us to a later date while they got their evidence together to prove that the smuggling had been going on for some time. They ignored my questions.

I looked across at my solicitor, silently urging him to intervene on this meaningless charade of endless "no comments". He leaned forward: "Officers, my client has clearly indicated his intention not to comment at interview and I don't think that it is going to help anyone make progress by continuing with this futile line of questioning. Unless you can adduce some evidence that my client can respond to, I suggest that you bail my client and his girlfriend to come back here in one month's time."

The thin, intense, dark-haired guy from Revenue & Customs had pretty much left Dickinson to deal with the interview thus far, but he now leaned forward, looking directly at me. He spoke softly but clearly and his intense expression and controlled manner were unsettling.

"We don't think that this was your first trip Mr Luttrell. We think that we have unearthed a major smuggling ring defrauding Her Majesty's Government of millions of pounds of tax revenue. We have information to suggest that you have also been smuggling drugs, people and weapons into the UK via continental Europe. You have been laundering the criminal proceeds through Guernsey's banks. The fraudulent evasion of excise duty is just the start of it. Under the Proceeds of Crime Act 2002 we can seize all of the proceeds of suspected criminal activity. We don't need proof to do that, just reasonable suspicion. If you are found not guilty, you have to apply to recover the monies from us, not the other way around. We can also, in addition, levy a financial penalty of 100% of the duty due. A double whammy."

He went on: "The seriousness of this well organised and sophisticated criminal activity is clearly an attempt to cheat the public revenue, for which a maximum sentence of life imprisonment is possible". I stared at him in disbelief, before he continued:

"We know all of the links in the chain Mr Luttrell. We know who you are involved with and how long it has been going on. We will produce witness statements and photographic evidence of Class A drug hauls, weapons shipments and people trafficking." "These are indictable offences carrying long custodial sentences Mr Luttrell." He sat back in his chair, unblinking eyes scrutinising my reaction.

I tried not to show it, but I was shocked. Had those involved in the delivery of cigarettes to me been involved in something far worse? I sat in silence and began to doubt the cargoes that I had carried - had there been something else inside? Couldn't be, surely those I sold them to would have raised it with me? Had I been played a fool?

While my mind whirled, my solicitor responded: "My client has been in custody for around 18 hours and I shouldn't need to remind you, Officer Dickinson or you, Officer Howe, that the normal maximum period of detention without charge is 24 hours. Either you come up with some evidence to support these wild claims and charge my client, or you let my client and his girlfriend go."

Officer Howe opened his file and slowly and deliberately placed a piece of paper on the desk. My solicitor leaned forward and moved it closer to where we could both read it. It was an order from a High Court Judge extending the period for detention without charge to 96 hours.

They switched off the recording machine that had been taping the interview and showed us out. The short walk back to the holding suite with my solicitor was undertaken in silence.

CHAPTER 7

The cell door was shut behind us. My solicitor wheeled around to face me and angrily barked: "I suggest, Mr Luttrell, that it would be in your best interests to be frank with me. I can protect your interests better if I am not placed in a position where I am hijacked by accusations of serious crime. That order extending your custody is pretty rare, used only in terrorist matters or where serious, organised crime is involved and the Judge can be persuaded of such. I think you had better level with me."

I stared blankly at his face. My mind furiously imagined scenarios where I was dragged into actions taken by my suppliers without my knowledge. I could be made a scapegoat so easily, a patsy even. A convincing record of multiple Channel trips over a long period of time and more cash in a Guernsey bank account than most serious criminals could ever hope to amass in a lifetime. It had been too easy. I was in the shit.

"Listen, I don't know what they are talking about. Something is not right here. I am being set up. Leave me to think and I will request that you attend if they try to interview me again." He nodded, handed me his card and banged on the cell door for the custody sergeant to let him out.

Despite the shock, I felt bone tired. We had been arrested about 10.30 am, it was now 5.30 the next morning and I had slept for twenty minutes at most. I lay down on the bench and instantly fell into a troubled sleep.

The cell door clanging open woke me and I didn't immediately remember where I was. Officer Howe had come in and shut the door. I struggled to focus my eyes on his tightly drawn face. He approached me, his face closing in on mine, uncomfortably close.

"You are a fucking idiot Luttrell. You are going to jail for a very long time. We will confiscate every penny you have. I hope that you had a good time with Miss Neilsen because she is the last woman you are going to see for a very long time. You will get life imprisonment. So will she."

I tried to surface from the pull of deep sleep and focus on what he was saying. He went on:

"We know that you have been an intrinsic part of one of the biggest, most organised and longstanding major criminal operations that we have ever discovered. You and your fellow conspirators have trafficked underage girls into prostitution, been one of the major sources of Class A drugs into this country and laundered millions of pounds."

He was still leaning over me, invading my space. "You are the tip of an iceberg, the only arrest made so far, but we know, and are starting to amass evidence of, what lies out of sight." "We have found the residue of cocaine and some heroin in the lockers of your boat.

We have intelligence to suggest that over 5 kilograms of cocaine is currently stored in your boatyard. I have shipping manifestos and photographs detailing the hundreds of Eastern Europeans that you have trafficked into this country in the last three years. He straightened up, paced away from me before abruptly turning to face me. "If it isn't so, we will make it so".

He walked closer. His face was now just inches from mine, his stale breath washing over my face. I stood up. "This is crazy, all I have done is smuggle a few duty free cigarettes. You are trying to fit me up for something that I didn't do. I want my solicitor here. Now!" He shook his head, ignoring my request and continued:

"We can produce evidence showing you to have made over 150 cross-channel trips in the last three years. We *will* find cocaine in your boatyard and we already have scientific reports showing cocaine powder and heroin residue in your boat's lockers. Your cigarette supplier will attest to the fact that you also took delivery from them of drugs, weapons and young prostitutes and smuggled them into the UK. Your girlfriend has lived in Guernsey during those three years and we can produce mobile telephone records detailing calls made to your suppliers, pretty much weekly. The apartment that you rented at St Peter Port contained a handwritten record of many of the shipments and we found cocaine residue all over the kitchen work surfaces. There was marijuana in the bedside table. Heroin residue was found in the bathroom. You have over £1.2million in cash sitting in a bank account in Guernsey. I suggest that you sit and think about that for a while, instead of crying out for your fucking lawyer."

He slammed the door. It wasn't cold in that cell, but I shivered.

When you get accused of something you didn't do, you start to open up a mental parallel universe in which you really did what they say. You really did import hard drugs. You did traffic women and guns. You are part of a major smuggling operation and a member of a powerful criminal gang. I shook my head, as if to clear it. I hadn't done any of those things. I was being set up, but how could I disprove a negative? I had no doubt he would "find" the evidence that he described and I had absolutely no doubt that the overall picture the prosecution would paint at Court was going to put me in jail for a very long time. The contents of every bank account confiscated. Separated from Vilda and likely her wrongly punished and imprisoned too. Our perfect world crashing down.

CHAPTER 8

I fell into a fitful sleep, frequently waking from this shallow sleep with terrors of prison cells and a lengthy court case running through my mind. The result of which would be my inevitable guilt and long incarceration. It was almost a relief to be woken by the custody sergeant at 8 am and given some breakfast - a couple of slices of toast and a mug of luke-warm tea. I asked him: "Can I speak to Vilda?"

"No Sir. You will not be allowed to communicate with her while you are in custody. You can request a further consultation with your lawyer, if you so wish, but I understand that there is no intention to undertake a further interview until all of the evidence has been pieced together. We can hold you for three more days without charge and in a case as complex and serious as this, I would fully expect that you won't be interviewed again until the end of that time limit." I stared into the distance.

He went on: "You can take a shower and I will bring you some fresh clothing shortly. You do have the right to consult with your solicitor by phone. Do you want to speak with your lawyer?"

I shook my head. "No, that's fine. I'll just wait it out." I took a shower and looked out for Vilda on my return to the holding suite, but saw no-one. I paced the cell like room, running over the events of the last 24 hours again and again in my mind. I was left undisturbed in the cell for the rest of that day. Meals and the occasional drink being the only interruption to the gloom and monotony.

Around 9pm that evening I had just settled onto the padded bench, trying to get comfortable and resigned to another night there when I heard the lock turning in the door. Officer Howe came in and I sat up expectantly. He closed the door behind him.

"Luttrell, we have just about finished collating your file and the next step is to discuss with the Crown Prosecution Service what you and Miss Neilsen will be charged with. This is going to be an extensive prosecution and will lead to a trial at Crown Court. The CPS will also give me their view on whether or not I will be successful in the application that I am going to make to Court to deny you bail. Your lifestyle and financial situation place you in a position to abscond from bail very easily and I am not going to take that risk. If you remain in custody, which is my intention, you will then be brought to trial within a month."

I jumped to my feet. I felt myself losing control and shouted: "This is a crock of shit and you know it. I want to see the evidence that you claim to have and I will go through it with my lawyer. You know as well as I do that all I did was evade tax duty on some cigarettes. A fine and a slap on the wrist, that's all."

Howe shoved me roughly back on to the bench. His

eyes wide and nostrils flaring as he shouted: "You are likely to be charged with importation of Class A drugs in substantial quantities. I have surveillance records of over 150 cross Channel trips. We have witness statements from several illegal immigrants who have been trafficked for sex. They state that they were brought to this country on your boat. They describe your boat in detail and name it. We have obtained disclosure from your bank on Guernsey showing regular credits to your account amounting to well over 1.2 million pounds. We have also obtained details of a further Channel Islands' account in which some 7-8 million euros have passed through, from and to various destinations that we can link to organised crime."

He stared straight at me, daring me to challenge him. He continued: "You are going to prison for a very long time and I will personally ensure that every single penny in your accounts is confiscated as proceeds of crime. All of your other assets will be seized. I have also established your means of supplying drugs and sex workers nationally through your warehouse in Hereford and your cousin's involvement in the distribution network. Over the next twenty four hours or so I will have firmly established links between you and a large international criminal organisation, whose members, as we speak, are to be made subject to a European Arrest Warrant. I will personally offer them immunity from prosecution if they testify against you in Court."

My head was reeling. I just sat back on the bench and tried to make some sense of what I was hearing.

Officer Howe moved away from the door and sat across the room from me. He lowered his voice; "The

Custody Officer changes shift at nine and there is no record of this visit to you. You haven't requested that a solicitor is present and what I am about to say is between you and me. I will deny the visit, let alone that this conversation ever happened. Do you follow? I lifted my head and stared into his dark, lifeless eyes.

"Simon, I can help you through this. I have enough evidence to put you away for a long time and secure myself a promotion at the same time. This will be a major prosecution. But so far, I haven't shared my evidence with the CPS and it is only known to my team. Officer Dickinson was the arresting officer, but all he has seen, first hand, is your smuggling of cigarettes. I requested that he hand over your case to me and my team. I now have full authority over this prosecution. Do you understand?" I nodded, unsure where this was going but grasping eagerly at this seeming chink of light.

"My team from HM Revenue & Customs consists of me and four people seconded from the NSA, which is the National Security Agency of the European Union. The UK Government fully co-operates with Brussels on countering cross-border criminal activity. We are part of a larger inter-governmental task force working on enforcing the EU Common Security & Defence Policy objectives, including crisis management and civil and military operations. All on behalf of the European Union. We answer to the European Council, not domestic governments."

"It sounds like you guys have a lot of fun, but I don't understand what any of this has to do with me?"

"Simon, what I am about to say to you, never got

said. Do you understand?" He looked for my assurance and I nodded.

"You don't read about it in the papers because it would cause widespread alarm and panic, but Europe is going to suffer an acute food shortage within the next two years, maximum. Globalisation has enabled Europe to consume more food than it produces for some time now. The current situation is unsustainable because growing populations in excess producing countries will shortly mean that domestic consumption demands will turn that food surplus into a deficit. The West will either starve or, more likely, pay large sums of money to take away the food produced in other countries, meaning that their populations will starve." He paused. "That doesn't have to be the case."

I took stock for a while, trying to follow the unexpected direction of travel. "OK, but what does this have to do with me?"

"The nation states within the European Union could easily grow enough food and rear sufficient livestock to feed all 500 million Europeans and have a surplus to export to a wider, hungry world. The reason we don't is because the European Commission has been stymied every time that we try to authorise the introduction of high yielding crops and food stuffs. The nation states just can't face tackling the public opposition to genetically modified crops. They are thwarting the Commission's steps to introduce those crops. Crops that would easily double the current levels of agricultural production. The UK Government is the worst offender and, in pandering to a bunch of sceptics and deniers who don't even look at the science, it is holding the rest of Europe back. We are so fucking arrogant that we are going to let people starve."

I nodded. "I follow you, but I still don't get it. Why on earth are you mentioning this to me?"

"Simon, I am going to make you an offer. I could drop this thing right here, right now. I would make sure that you and your petty little smuggling racket are left in peace. I can stop this prosecution before it even starts, but in return you must do something for me. If you have an ounce of public duty in you, which I doubt, you might even take some satisfaction in doing this because it will be defeating hunger and starvation. It will make Europe safer. You are going to carry something for me on the next smuggling trip that you make. All I ask is that you take a half ton of high yielding grass seed which I will arrange to be delivered to your boat mid-Channel. You will then return to the United Kingdom and mix that high yielding grass seed with the seed that your cousin distributes nationally as part of his legitimate business interests. That is it. That is all you have to do."

I stared at him blankly, genuinely bewildered.

"If you agree to do this, I will bail you and Vilda for a month. I will put a stay on the Mareva Injunction currently being obtained against your bank accounts and assets. Everything on hold. You don't say a word to anyone. You do exactly what I tell you. You introduce the genetically modified seed to your cousin's supplies and carry on your life as before. I will ensure that insufficient evidence is produced to charge you. Your bail and Vilda's will lapse. It will be over. I'm offering you a get out of jail free card…. think about it!" He looked at me earnestly and headed for the door. Before going out he turned and said "I'll be back in the morning. You mention this to anyone and I will simply deny that I have even spoken with you and, remember, there will be no entry of my visit in the custody record. Sleep on it".

Sleep was the farthest thing from my mind. I was absolutely confident that the evidence he spoke of could be manufactured and used against me. It was so easy. My frequent trips and minor league smuggling gave them a base to build something far more serious and I didn't doubt that they could coerce other criminals to testify against me by offering some kind of plea bargain. I expect that his team had all sorts of information on many, many people and could choose to use it or lose it, depending upon their aims. I couldn't face losing the money that Vilda and I had saved up over the last three years, forcing us to abandon all of our plans when we were so close to realising them.

The alternative that he offered seemed so simple and without risk. All we had to do was undertake another of our now routine weekly trips and bring back some grass seed. I would then mix it with the seed Sean kept at his warehouse, with or without Sean's knowledge. It was easy. I shifted position on the cell bench. But was it too easy? I was facing a long spell in jail and the loss of a fortune and in the alternative all I had to do was act as a delivery boy for some crop seed and walk away, for ever. It was incredible!

I thought over the story that he had told me. He certainly seemed to passionately believe in what he was saying and I had picked up recent press coverage about public resistance to genetically modified crops generally and the fact that certain GM crops hadn't been accepted for use in the UK. The food shortage point also made sense. You would have to be blind not to notice that much of what was available on the supermarket's shelves came from overseas and it stood to reason that if it was available to us, then it was depriving someone somewhere else of it. The population was booming, everywhere, and I could follow his argument that without some kind of step change or paradigm shift in food production there would eventually be too little food being chased by too many people.

What I couldn't understand was how introducing half a ton of grass seed into the UK food chain was going to make the slightest bit of difference? If that genetically modified grass seed was mixed with normal grass seed and then distributed all over the UK and planted then surely it would take decades for it to have any real effect? It would have to cross-fertilise with the normal seed and then spread in order for it to meaningfully increase the yield of grass nationally in the UK. That could only take decades.

I thought and thought about it, lying in that poky cell in the dark. I would like to have discussed it with Vilda and my mind wandered briefly to her. I wondered how she was holding up. I figured that she had kept to a "no-comment" interview and hoped that she had then been left alone in her cell until this secret deal was put to me.

I reckoned that Officer Howe knew that I was going to accept it. For all my misgivings, it was simply one day out of my life doing what they wanted and in return we both walked free and onwards to the next stage in our lives. Was it too good to be true? Probably, but what choice did I have? The more I thought about it, the clearer the real purpose of their plot became. My guess was that the covert introduction of the GM grass seed would allow them to railroad the public and opposition groups into later accepting it. All they had to do was one day find evidence of genetically modified grass growing in the UK and the whole argument against it fell apart. It would be like closing the stable door after the horse had bolted. Once it was here, and spreading, what was the point of opposing its widespread use?

I imagined that they would track where the seed was going to be used and then fund a university or agricultural college to study the grass growing in those areas under some pretence or other. Lo and behold, if they didn't find that genetically modified crops were already growing in the UK!

I was sure that was it. I considered what that meant for me and Vilda. I ran through in my head how what he was proposing would work. We had to do a further smuggling trip, bring back the seed and distribute it. Easy. But then what? Would they let us just walk away, simple as that? I couldn't see why not as it would be simpler for everyone. I reckoned that the grass seed we were to carry was going to look just like any other grass seed. After we had mixed it and distributed it, all trace of the subterfuge would be gone. Vilda and I couldn't turn whistle-blowers as there would be no proof and to do so we would have to admit to a history of smuggling which would put us back into facing the same scenario - jail and confiscation of all of our money and assets. It wasn't a case of them trusting us, more a case of them having nothing to fear. There was nothing that we could do.

But could we trust them? How extreme were they and how far would they be prepared to go? Alone in that dark cell, it was pretty easy to become paranoid. The situation we found ourselves in was so unbelievable already that it didn't take too many mental leaps of my fevered mind to think we might personally be in real danger after we had carried out their wishes. Wouldn't they want us out of the way after their mission had been accomplished? Wouldn't it be less risky for them?

I ran it over again and again in my mind. I kept coming back to the fact that for us to act as whistle-blowers would only serve to put us in jail and destroy all of our dreams - they must have thought that through. I was also comforted by the fact that we had been arrested and he spoke of us being released on bail. There was and always would be a hard, real record of that and if we simply disappeared or were killed then an investigation would be made. Questions would be asked, it couldn't just be hushed up. What he proposed, about the bail being cancelled because insufficient evidence being found, would work for everyone. Vilda and I could walk away and there would be no further questions asked. I guessed the authorities placed lots of people on bail that they didn't eventually charge. It was probably more common than not.

My mind was made up. I quickly drifted into a deep, untroubled sleep.

I woke as the custody sergeant brought me breakfast on a metal tray the next morning. I tried to make seemingly light, innocent conversation. "You look tired Sergeant, is your shift nearly over?" He put down the tray. "I'm out of here at 9am, when the next duty Sergeant will come on. You will have to speak to him about what the plan is for you today as I haven't heard anything."

I nodded and asked him the time. It was 7.30 am and I was sure Officer Howe would come to see me at 9. I figured that he was going to take advantage of the handover between custody sergeants to pay another unauthorised and unrecorded visit to my cell. I knew what I would say. Vilda and I would be bailed and released. I looked forward to getting back to the boatyard and some fresh air.

CHAPTER 9

At 9am Officer Howe entered my cell almost noise-lessly. He carefully shut the cell door. We moved to the back of the room, furthest from the custody suite. "Have you thought about what we discussed?" I nodded. "I agree to what you ask, but I want your assurance that after we have done as you request that Vilda and I will be left alone. We will do everything that you have asked but then we must be able to walk away, our bail cancelled and the bank account untouched."

He looked earnestly at me and spoke softly: "If you carry out what I have asked, you will not hear from me again. You will receive a letter from Border Force notifying you that your bail has been cancelled. You can carry on with your lives as they were before. But, and this is a very big but, you must carry out our instructions to the letter. We will place you under surveillance every step of the way, just to make sure. We need to know that the operation has been successful, no hiccups, no problems, no difficulties. If we are satisfied, then you will never hear from us again. It goes without saying that you must never reveal what has been done or said, to anyone ever." He paused for a while. "Now, are we in agreement?"

I looked him in the eye and he looked straight back, unflinching. I nodded. "In an hour or so the custody sergeant will fetch you and process your release. Officer Dickinson will set out the terms of your bail and bail you back here to a date in one month's time. I will authorise the immediate release of your boat and you and Vilda can take it back to Salcombe. Today."

He paced up and down in the cell, before saying: "I have some arrangements to make. When are you due to pick up your next consignment of cigarettes from the French fisherman?"

"Tuesday morning. Vilda will need to call him to confirm, but he will be expecting to rendez-vous, as usual, at 10.00 am on Tuesday next. We always meet at Dixcart Bay on Sark. That gives us four days. How do we play it from here?"

Howe thought for a while, then said: "Once you have been released, go home and act normally. As soon as I have made the arrangements, I will contact you there. Don't leave Salcombe unless it is absolutely necessary and make sure that you are alone each night. I will come to your boatyard one evening and talk through what will happen and what must be done."

"I want you to send Miss Neilsen back to Guernsey as soon as possible. There will be a flight from Exeter Airport tomorrow, make sure that she is on it. I haven't spoken to her about this. She was interviewed but chose not to comment and hasn't been spoken to since. Do not tell her of our conversation. The fewer people that know of our arrangements the better, for all of us. She will be told that there is currently insufficient evidence to charge her and she will be bailed on the same terms and to the same date as you are. I don't want her or anyone else on your boat when you take delivery of our package. Do you understand?"

I wasn't expecting that. I had anticipated carrying the last shipment with Vilda, delivering it to Hereford, carrying out their instructions and then the two of us disappearing together. For good. However, Vilda didn't need to know and why expose her to something of this nature unnecessarily? I looked him in the eye and said: "OK, that's fine. I'll do just as you ask. I'll wait to hear from you in Salcombe." He turned, carefully opened the cell door, and was gone.

CHAPTER 10

I walked, blinking, into the sunlight. As Howe had predicted, after an hour or so I had been taken from my cell and stood before the custody sergeant. Officer Dickinson was there too and he gave me a bail notice, requiring me to return in one month, pending "further enquiries". He didn't look very happy about it, but made no comment.

As I descended the steps of the Border Force building, I saw Vilda standing on the pavement. Her face was drawn and there were dark smudges under her eyes. I took her in my arms and told her that everything was going to be OK. She smiled weakly and I said to her: "They have released the boat. Let's go to the boatyard and get away from all this."

I steered her towards the Border Force berth in the naval base, where they had moored the impounded boat. I showed the bail notices to a Border Force official and we were walked to the boat, after he had checked the details on his radio.

The boat was clean and the lockers were as we had left them, minus the cigarettes. I handed a sailing jacket to Vilda, fired up the diesels and we cast off.

As we cleared the naval base, I let the boat drift in mid-channel and turned and kissed Vilda. Tears were rolling down her cheeks, somehow pale despite her tan.

"We can relax now darling. Trust me, everything will be fine. I told you. All that we are going to get is a fine and a slap on the wrist. They would have charged us if they had known about all of the previous trips. We've got away with it."

She dried her eyes and a smile returned to her beautiful face. "I'm just going to head over to Gosport Marina, just on the other side over there, to fill up with diesel and then let's head back to Salcombe. I want a shower, good coffee and to lie in bed with you - it doesn't have to be in that particular order?" She smiled. "We have been in a custody suite for over 48 hours with no change of underwear and if you think you are coming near me until you have showered, you are very much mistaken!"

I filled up at the marina, while Vilda grabbed some sandwiches and drinks. It was probably over one hundred miles to Salcombe from Portsmouth by boat. We would have to run between the Isle of Wight and the mainland, heading west, and then follow the coast until Weymouth when we could go further offshore to cross Exeter bay. I would normally have broken the journey up and stopped off along the way. Perhaps Lyme Regis, taking in the Jurassic coastline, but I just wanted to get back.

It took us a little over 3 hours as the sea was quite rough and I kept well offshore to avoid the worst of it. By the time the familiar sight of Bolt Head at the mouth of Salcombe estuary came into view, I was tired of standing and we both looked a little knocked around. I throttled back and cruised gently up the estuary.

As the speed dropped, it became possible to talk to each other again and I said to Vilda: "It's 3.45pm. Steve and Andy will still be working at the boatyard. I'll take the boat around to the pontoon at the back of the boatyard and we can let ourselves in through the back. Let's just tell them that we have had a couple of days in Guernsey and that we have only just returned from there. We don't have to say anything more and you go up to the sail loft while I catch up with them on what has been going on at the yard. Put the kettle on and run a bath and I will be up as soon as I can." She nodded and we stepped on to the pontoon, rolling slightly until we got used to being back on terra firma.

I had converted the sail loft above the boat yard into my living space shortly after buying the boat yard. Nobody made sails locally anymore and the ceiling height and dimensions of the loft made an excellent open plan apartment. I climbed up the wooden steps to the sail loft and closed the hatch to the floor.

There was a steaming cup of coffee waiting for me on the kitchen counter and I walked with it, supping carefully, to the bathroom at the end of the loft. I poked my head around to find Vilda lying in the bath surrounded by candles, her eyes closed. I took off my clothes, dropping them to the floor, and climbed in behind her. I took a bar of soap and gently massaged her shoulders, kissing her lightly on the neck. She lay back against me and we gently made love, warm, secure and finally able to relax.

After snoozing for a while in the bath, we dried

ourselves and collapsed into bed. We slept for hours. It was dark outside when I woke and I carefully extricated myself from under the duvet and padded naked to the kitchen, leaving Vilda asleep. I fixed us an omelette and brought it to the bed on a tray. I kissed her eyelids gently and her blue eyes opened slowly. We eat in bed in silence, hungrier than I can remember being for a long time.

After we had finished, I set the tray on the floor and said "Listen Angel, we need to talk about what we are going to do next from here". Her head was on my chest and I stroked her hair. "I am going to drive you to Exeter Airport in the morning and I want you to fly back to Guernsey, book yourself into a hotel. I've got some things that I need to sort out here and I will then take the boat over to you on Monday afternoon. I want you to call Edouard and arrange for me to rendez-vous with him at 10 am on Tuesday morning. I am going to take one last shipment from him and then tell him that it's over and that we are moving away. Once the last run is done, I'll meet you in Mallorca and we can start to build our life together."

I felt her body stiffen and she sat up, eyes wide and furious. "Are you fucking crazy? We are already on bail for smuggling and you want to do one last run? Are you out of your mind?"

I turned my face away from her and said: "I have to settle things with Edouard and with Sean. I need to pay them and bring this whole operation to a close. Remember, neither of them know that we have been arrested. Edouard will have a shipment waiting for me and will get spooked if I don't take it. He might cause trouble. Sean's buyers will be expecting the cigarettes and he will need to give them some notice that there aren't going to be further deliveries. They will need to make alternative arrangements. Sean will be wondering why there hasn't been a delivery this week and I want to tell him face to face what has happened. I'll do this one last trip and square it all away. Then we just walk away. For good."

She pulled the duvet up around her shoulders and glared at me. "If that is what you want to do then it is up to you, but I want nothing to do with it. I'll go to Guernsey and fix things up with Edouard but I am not going to play any further part. You can do the delivery on your own". I nodded. "That's fine, I'll meet Edouard alone and bring the shipment back myself. You fly on to Mallorca and I will meet you there as soon as I have delivered it to Sean's warehouse and had a chance to speak with him."

Her face was angry and her eyes blazed. "Have you forgotten that we are on bail? If you get caught making another shipment, they will cancel your bail - mine too probably - and keep you in custody. Do we really need to take that risk?"

"Hey, hey, calm down. I am not going to get caught, I'll be careful. Let's just do as I say and within a week we will be drinking Rioja in a beach bar in Mallorca, watching the sun go down. I promise. Trust me." I squeezed her hand. She turned and faced the wall, pulling most of the duvet with her. The Scandinavian cold shoulder.

In the morning I made breakfast in bed. Vilda didn't touch it. The journey to the airport was passed in total silence. I dropped her at the doors to the departure terminal and pulled her towards me for a kiss goodbye. She bit my lip, stared me hard in the face and disappeared into the terminal building.

CHAPTER 11

It was two days before Officer Howe paid me a visit.

He arrived late on the Saturday night, on foot, dressed in civilian clothes. Deck shoes, brown moleskins, a blue yachting jacket and a sailing cap, the visor pulled down and partially obscuring his rat like face. Indistinguishable from just about every other male wandering around Salcombe on a wet, windy Saturday night. I led him through the unlit boat showroom, up the steps to the sail loft. I closed the hatch. I nervously asked: "Can I get you anything? Tea, coffee?" He nodded, but didn't specify which. Coffee it was - I wanted a clear head to take in all the detail of the handover.

"Simon, I would expect that you aren't stupid enough to tape this conversation, are you?" He raised his eyebrows at me. I reassured him: "No, of course not, I just want this thing done and over". He quickly frisked my clothing. Officer Howe nodded: "Good, I hope that this will be the last time that we meet. If you do what I say, then by the middle of the week it will all be over and your life can resume its normal course. On Tuesday morning I want you to meet the French fisherman in the usual place at the usual time. I want everything to be the same as normal, except, as I said, Miss Neilsen will not be with you." I nodded and he went on: "Do you think that will seem unusual to the fisherman?"

"No, he won't be alarmed or suspicious. It has been that way before. I have often done runs singlehandedly. He won't even question it. I expect that we will chat about the weather and Edouard's fishing prospects and then he will hand over the cigarettes in return for payment." Howe nodded. "What if the weather is bad, will he still come? Will you be able to make the crossing?"

"My RIB-X can handle anything that the Channel can throw at it, no problem. The trip back, when the boat is laden, might be a little slower if the waves cut up rough but it won't present a challenge. As far as Edouard is concerned, he fishes in the protected coastal waters and has fished them all of his life. He always puts out to sea, whatever the weather. It would be a matter of pride. In any event, the long range forecast is good. Cloudy but dry, a moderate sea and little wind. Maybe some fog, but I have GPS on the boat."

Howe responded: "Good. I have arranged for a small Border Force launch to be patrolling around the Channel Islands on Tuesday, manned only by members of my team. They won't attract attention, but they will be watching you. Will you depart from Salcombe early on Tuesday morning or stay overnight on Monday in Guernsey?"

I paused and thought for a while. "I am going to take the RIB over on Monday afternoon, stay in a hotel with Vilda on Monday night and then pop over to Sark in the morning. She is shaken up by what happened and upset with me for planning one more trip. I don't blame her, in the circumstances. She doesn't want to accompany me and I can understand why. I have told her that I will do it alone and that it will be the last trip. The end of it."

"Good, I repeat that I want you alone on that boat. My team won't approach you if there is anyone with you." I nodded. "Once you have made the handover with Edouard, I don't want you to return to Guernsey, instead you will proceed without stopping to Salcombe. What route would you usually take?"

"I'll meet Edouard at Dixcart Bay - the bay where we were arrested - on Sark and then head east, anti-clockwise around Sark. When I get to the Northern tip of the island, it is pretty much a straight run home across the Channel, maintaining the same bearing until I reach the mouth of Salcombe's estuary. That's the usual route. If I need fuel or food I sometimes pop in to St Peter Port on Guernsey on the way back, but for this trip I will make sure that the boat is fully fuelled before the rendez-vous with Edouard."

Howe took a sip of his coffee and replied: "That is fine, but this time I want you to head west after the rendez-vous and circle Sark in a clockwise direction before heading for Herm. Do you know it?"

I nodded. "Yes, it's in the channel between Guernsey and Sark, next to another little island called Jethou, isn't it? Howe nodded and I went on. "I haven't stopped there before but I usually head just south of those islands when I make the trip from St Peter Port to Sark. Close enough to see them. They are pretty much uninhabited, aren't they?"

Howe shook his head. "No, there are residents there, but not many. It's only harbour is on the west coast and nearly all of the settlements are on that side of the island. I want you to stick to the east coast and head up to Shell Beach - its midway up the east coast and the first beach you come to. Anchor in ten metres or so of water and wait for my team to join you."

He looked for my acknowledgement and I nodded. He continued: "We want you to carry 500 kilograms of grass seed, can you and your boat manage that?"

I paused. "How will it be packaged? If it is in one bale then it will be too heavy to lift and we would need to rig a davit to transfer it from boat to boat."

Howe took a final gulp of his coffee and replied: "No, it will be in hermetically sealed, water proof packets weighing 10 kilograms each, fifty of them. Each packet is about the size of a large breakfast cereal box. How will you securely stow them? They need to be out of sight and it is imperative that they are not damaged or spilt, obviously."

I took a large gulp of my now luke-warm coffee and pondered on it. "The forward locker on my RIB would be pretty much filled by the cigarettes, but I could perhaps fit ten seed packets in there. If I remove the second row of seats, then I could store the remaining 40 packets on the deck. It's non-slip and well protected by the RIB's tubing. I could lash them down with a tarpaulin and…"

Howe interrupted me before I could finish. He leant forward earnestly, his face close to mine. "No, they must be more secure than that. They must not move about in transit, they could be damaged. It is absolutely imperative that the sealed packaging is not ruptured. I will arrange for them to be put in padded crates, ten of them. Remove your rear seating before you make the trip in order to make space for the crates. Bring lines to secure the crates in position. Lash them to the rear bulkhead. My team can help you get each crate on board your boat, but how will you unload them without being seen when you get to Salcombe?"

"I'll bring the RIB to the pontoon behind the boat-yard. I would normally leave the cargo on-board until its dark and then bring them ashore. I usually load the cigarettes straight into my car but it will be too heavy this time. I can use the twin-cab truck from the boatyard. I'll load the crates into the flat bed and then pull over the tonneau cover - it's waterproof and secure, it will also keep them out of sight." Howe nodded.

I went on: "If the crates are too heavy for me to bring ashore then I will have to do it packet by packet. It will take some time but I can reverse the truck through the boatyard right up to the pontoon. No one will see." "That's fine" Howe confirmed.

"What should I do with them when I get to the warehouse in Hereford?"

"We know the layout of the warehouse. There are five large hoppers full of grass seed, aren't there?" I nodded. "I want you to empty ten packets into each of the hoppers. Mix it up thoroughly with the existing seed using a stick or something. They need to be well mixed in. When your cousin draws seed from a hopper for a delivery, we want plenty of our seed to go with each delivery. How will you do that without your cousin becoming aware?"

I stood up and paced around the loft. "I have a key to the warehouse and I know the alarm code. It will be tiring, but I can load the seed into my truck as soon as it gets dark on Tuesday evening and then drive up to Hereford and deliver the seed into the hoppers that night. Sean never visits the warehouse at night time, he likes to get back home to see his children before their bedtime."

Howe was silent for a while. "That sounds fine. You should know that you will be watched every step of the way. I want you to take the same route up the Wye Valley that you took when you were being followed." His eyes met mine and narrowed. "Yes that was us. Be under no illusion. You follow what we have just agreed to the letter, do you understand? If you deviate from the plan, change your timings, take a different route, anything…we will know and the deal is off. You will be re-arrested and charged. You will go to jail for a very long time."

I felt sick momentarily and shook my head to clear it. "I understand, I will do exactly as you have asked." I thought for a while. "What if I need to contact you, if arrangements need to change or something?"

"Make sure they don't. Anyway, we will be watching you the whole time, from cradle to grave, as it were. If you do anything wrong, rest assured, we will intervene."

I showed him out, not in the least bit sorry to see him go. I didn't like him, he made my skin crawl, but that didn't matter. I would follow the plan and in a few days it would all be over.

I called Vilda before I went to bed. At least she

was speaking to me now. She had already spoken to Edouard and Tuesday's rendez-vous had been confirmed. Not long now baby, not long.

CHAPTER 12

Sunday morning I rose early and went to check on the RIB. I pumped the tubes, washed down the deck and checked the battery charge and oil levels. I didn't want any problems on the next trip. I removed the rear row of seats, as Howe had directed, and placed them in one of the yard's storage rooms. I fired up the engines, released the mooring lines and crossed over the estuary to the fuel barge.

It was a beautiful, bright day and the estuary looked picture postcard perfect in the morning sunshine. I was delayed on my return from the fuel barge by a fleet of yawls tacking up the estuary. I let the RIB drift as they criss-crossed in front of me through the water, their brightly coloured wooden hulls still visible long after the race numbers on the white sails could no longer be deciphered. I gently brought the RIB alongside the pontoon and tied her off. She was all set for the trip to Guernsey on Tuesday, I just needed to stow some bottles of water and headed to the boatyard for them.

I stepped off the pontoon through the gap in the wall into the boatyard. I stopped in my tracks. The large wooden gates that gave access onto the road were open and a grey VW panel van had reversed in and parked. There was no-one in the cab. The rear compartment had windows but they were darkly tinted. I approached the van from the side and placed my hands on the window of the sliding door, leaning my forehead against the glass to try to see in. As my eyes were adjusting to the dark, I was grabbed from behind and put in an armlock. At the same time the sliding door opened and a leg flicked out, kicking me in the solar plexus. I doubled-up forward into the van, my assailant pushing me in from behind. I was on the floor, fighting for breath as the van pulled away.

I lifted my head to try to get a glimpse of my assailants but my head was forced into the floor of the van. "Don't move. Try to take shallow breaths - you have been winded. If you don't struggle, we won't have to hurt you again. Lie still for ten minutes, there is somebody who wants to talk with you." The deep voice was calm, measured and commanding.

I did what he said. I didn't have much of a choice. As my eyes became accustomed to the gloom I could see nothing but the floor of the van. It was so clean that I doubted if the van had ever been used before. I tried to gauge the direction of travel but was so disorientated that all I could make out was that we were heading uphill, out of Salcombe.

As my breath returned, I shouted "What the fuck is going on, who are you guys?" "Just sit tight and keep quiet. You won't be harmed, our boss wants to talk to you. Five minutes more and we will be there." They hadn't spoken one word to each other, but I was being held against the floor with my arms pinned behind my back. I couldn't move an inch, not even to lift my head. I could hear their calm, slow breathing contrasting with my rapid gulps for air.

I could tell from the crashing ride that we were driving at speed along a country lane. The van rolled and dived, but the pressure of their grip on me didn't change. I decided to lay still, which was pragmatic of me because there really wasn't anything else that I could do. After a couple of minutes the van slowed and one of my assailants got out, leaving the sliding door open. He must have been opening gates as moments later I felt the van turn off the road and heard the gates shut behind us.

I was pulled through the sliding door of the van and lifted to my feet. I squinted until my eyes grew accustomed to the sunlight. I was in a farmyard with an open fronted barn in front of me and a stone farmhouse to my right. I was marched towards the door of the farmhouse, my arms still gripped behind my back by one large hand. His other arm wrapped tightly around my chest. I am 180 cm and pretty well built, but he virtually carried me into the farmhouse, my feet barely touching the floor.

"Sit down Mr Luttrell. I apologise for the theatricals but we had to lift you quickly and quietly, without being seen." He was seated at the pine kitchen table. He was tall and slim, long legs crossed, his hands behind his head as he reclined. A grey suit, black brogues and striped tie - sharply at odds with the rural surroundings. Greying hair and a lined face that spoke of imminent retirement, but his eyes were vivid and bright.

He held my gaze directly. I rather suspected that

those sharp blue eyes missed nothing. I approached the kitchen table and sat down opposite him. "Who are you and why have you brought me here? What the hell is going on?" I was angry. I had one dead arm and a stomach that felt like it had been kicked by a mule.

He leaned forward, placing both palms flat on the table. He spoke slowly and assuredly. "My name is Brown. I am the head of a counter terrorism unit within the Security Service, MI5. You are safe Mr Luttrell and I am sure it won't be necessary to strike you again. I apologise for that, it was imperative that we collected and processed you here without being seen. I have a considerable amount to say to you Mr Luttrell and it will, inevitably, feel something of a lecture but it is very important that you listen and understand. We need your help Mr Luttrell. I wouldn't ask for that without explaining why. I am a reasonable person. I believe that you will find it a compelling request." He stood up and began to slowly pace the room.

"On Tuesday morning you are sailing on that rather impressive boat of yours over to Guernsey. A repeat of many, many similar trips over the last couple of years, I understand. This time, however, you are returning with not just your illegal cargo, but a shipment of grass seed. This is at the request of Officer Howe of Her Majesty's Revenue & Customs, who has offered you a reward for doing so." He moved close to me. "One would imagine that he has promised to drop the investigation into your smuggling activities and to bring to an end the forthcoming prosecution?" He paused and glanced at me, the silence acting as an invitation for me to dispute his assumption. I didn't.

"What have you been told about your rather unusual cargo, Mr Luttrell?"

I squirmed in my seat. I didn't want to say anything that would threaten my arrangements with Howe. At the same time, it was clear that Brown already knew what was going to happen. It was inconceivable that he didn't already know why. I turned in my seat to face him, hoping to register any reaction that might show in that hitherto inscrutably calm face.

"I was told that I will be carrying a strain of genetically modified grass seed. It's to be introduced into the UK food chain." My voice trailed off slightly.

"I was told that unless high yielding genetically modified crops are grown in the UK, there will be a substantial food shortage in the very near future. Howe is part of a team that, ostensibly, works for the British Government but in reality is part of a task force from the National Security Agency of the European Union. He mentioned something about implementing European Union policy objectives, even if they were at odds with the wishes of domestic governments. It all sounded like political gobbledegook to me. I'd guess he is the kind of person who uses acronyms, refers to thought leadership and says "going forwards" a lot. Like the consultants who used to turn up and bore us to death when I was an officer in the Marines."

He nodded and smiled to himself, affecting to look out of the farmhouse window. "And what do you make of that Mr Luttrell?" "Well…, I haven't given it too much thought, I guess. If I don't do as he asks, I have been threatened with some serious charges that I have no way of disproving. A long jail sentence and all of my assets seized. I am not going to pretend that I agreed to go along with what he proposed out of some sense of altruism. It strikes me that for doing no real harm, possibly some good, I can get out of a situation that would otherwise ruin me and my plans for the future."

I shrugged and continued: "Let's face it, I am a relatively small time cigarette smuggler who has inadvertently got himself involved in something far bigger. I just want out. The quickest way possible."

He shook his head. "If only life were so simple, Mr Luttrell." He resumed his pacing, arms tucked behind his back like an earnest vicar about to deliver a sermon.

"The seeds you will be carrying were stolen from the Holcroft Institute three weeks ago. Have you heard of it?" I shook my head.

"The Holcroft Institute was formerly known as the Institute for Animal Health. A British research facility into virus diseases of farm animals and particularly viruses that can spread from animals to humans. Those seeds aren't genetically modified, but they are infected with the Foot & Mouth Virus. Their introduction into the UK's ecosystem will constitute the worst agroterrorism incident this country, for that matter the world, will have ever seen."

I jumped out of my chair. "You're fucking crazy, that's the most ludicrous thing I have ever heard".

"Do you remember the 2001 outbreak of Foot and Mouth?" I nodded. Brown continued: "That outbreak caused a crisis in British agriculture and tourism. Over 10 million sheep and cattle were slaughtered and it is estimated that the crisis cost the United Kingdom's economy over 8 billion pounds. It was only by a ruthlessly enforced lockdown on the movement of animals that the outbreak didn't become more widespread and the consequences even worse. In trying to identify the source of that outbreak the Holcroft Institute was tasked by the government with establishing whether contaminated animal feed could harbour and transmit the virus. Their research has established that it can and that the 2001 outbreak originated from a pig farmer in Northumberland feeding his animals untreated waste. Scientists being scientists, they went further. They posited that the virus could exist within agricultural crops and be transmitted when those crops were grown and, subsequently, consumed. Unfortunately, they proved that their hypothesis was correct and they purposefully infected a quantity of grass seed to help demonstrate the fact. That grass seed was recently stolen from their secure facility. If that seed is sown and animals feed on the resulting crop of grass, then they will be infected."

I banged the table. "Those sick bastards. They told me to mix that contaminated seed in with grass seed that is ordinarily delivered and sown throughout the UK. The outbreak will be nationwide. Why on earth would anyone want that to happen?"

"Because Mr Luttrell their intention is to create an outbreak of Foot & Mouth Virus that cannot be contained by a restriction on the movement of animals. The outbreak will affect animals in every region of the UK. Even if just one animal in each herd consumes grass from the contaminated seed, it will develop the virus and transmit it to the remaining animals in that herd. The UK will be gripped by a pandemic that it cannot understand or control. The only option, however unpalatable it may seem, will be the wholesale slaughter of every farm animal in the UK. The UK's economy will suffer catastrophically. We will become an impoverished nation. A nation reliant on foreign aid."

I stood up from the kitchen table in bewilderment. "But why would anyone want for that to happen? Nobody could be that evil. Who hates us that much? It's crazy! Who would be prepared to cause the slaughter of millions of animals? The UK will descend into chaos. Who hates us that much? Argentina, the IRA? Who?"

Brown opened an attaché case on the kitchen table. He handed me a bound document. "I think that perhaps you will need to sign this before I convince you of anything further. It is a non-disclosure agreement under the Official Secrets Act 1989 and I hereby formally notify you that what I have told you, and what I am about to tell you, is privileged information for the purposes of that legislation. Any disclosure of this information will be a criminal offence. Do you understand?" I nodded. He handed me a pen. I signed.

"I mentioned lecturing you earlier, Mr Luttrell. I am afraid that what I am about to tell you is going to sound very much like a lecture, but without it I don't feel that I can depend on your assistance." I stood up again. I must have looked like a jack-in-the-box. "Hold on a minute. I don't want any part of this. I just want my life to return to how it was. I don't want to hear this. I don't want to be involved."

"I am afraid that you *are* involved Mr Luttrell. I

wish it wasn't so, I really do. But the simple fact is that you have blundered into the most serious threat to our national security since the planned Nazi invasion of these islands during World War 2. We have identified the threat and we must deal with it. There is no alternative option." He turned to the two guys who had brought me here and who were standing either side of the farmhouse door. "Williams, Smith please go and make yourselves useful outside. Check that we are not being overheard. What I am about to say is beyond your present clearance levels. Please ensure that we are not interrupted."

He waited until the door closed before again sitting in front of me. His body seemed to crumple inward slightly and his face became pale. His eyes still burned fiercely though. He began.

"Have you ever heard of the Athena Mechanism?"

I shook my head, my face blank.

"It's a long story, but not an uninteresting one. It is the perfect demonstration of how a construct originally intended for peace can be subverted for evil. A cautionary tale, if you will. I will try to be as succinct as possible, but I think that a little historical context will assist. World War 2 resulted in such utter human and economic destruction that after 1945 there was a desire on behalf of all European politicians for its like to never happen again. The Treaty of Paris in 1951 was signed by France, West Germany and the Benelux countries and it introduced a community to integrate the coal and steel industries of Europe. Taking the industries needed to make weapons of war out of the hands of individual states and placing them into an international community was felt the safest way to ensure that no single country could ever again inflict such damage and destruction on its neighbours, or the world."

Brown wiped an imaginary speck of dirt from the kitchen table with his hand, before continuing. "From such noble beginnings sprang ever closer union between those countries and, at the same time, considerable enlargement until we have today's European Union. 28 member states. 500 million people. The process continued to accelerate and in 1992 the Maastricht Treaty was signed. I am not sure that the people of the United Kingdom were ever really made aware of what was being signed up to, but what we got was membership of a club whose ultimate aim was macroeconomic convergence and the creation of a federal states of Europe governed by a political elite unaligned to any one member state. A political elite not voted for by the people in those member states and accountable to no-one."

Notwithstanding forming the impression that I was back in a sixth form history lesson, I was more than intrigued to see where this was going. I nodded. "Go on."

"Closer fiscal integration was intended by the European Economic & Monetary Union and various treaties and policies resulted in the adoption of a common currency, the Euro, in 1999. The politicians were well on their way to achieving their ultimate dream, but it was no longer peace in Europe. The political elite had perverted the original honourable concept into something of a politician's wet dream - rule and control without the inconvenience of facing the threat of loss of office through democratic election. Democracy side-lined amid talk of global problems requiring global solutions. Their dream was being realised, slowly but surely. However, the enlargement of the European Union to include 28 member states has not come without its problems. They have sought to shackle together states with massively differing economic strengths into a single market and a single currency. The mercantilism those imbalances inevitably created has resulted in the crisis in the Eurozone that has plagued the EU member states in the last half decade. It has nearly torn the whole project apart."

My head was beginning to hurt. "I am struggling to stay with you, but how is all of this relevant to me?"

Brown continued: "I'll try to be succinct. The politicians decided that the only way out of the crisis was to converge all of the economies of the member countries into one European economy. Convergence became the pressure valve. If all the countries had the same economic strength then the disruptive pressures would be banished and the grand project would succeed."

I nodded. "I'm with you, so if everyone in the family gets the same pocket money as the eldest child then its happy families, right?"

"Quite so, but it hasn't happened. The richer member states cannot persuade their electorate to give away their hard earned money and wealth to the poorer ones. The attempt to converge the economies of the poorer nations with those of the richer has failed and demonstrably so. The economy of the UK, in particular, is just too strong. The UK, despite incredible international pressure to do so, has not adopted the Euro and so has retained more control over its own economy than the other member states. London's dominance as a financial centre has given us the wherewithal to undermine the Euro and the whole federalist European project itself. That is why they have developed the Athena Mechanism."

I interrupted: "I don't understand, what is the Athena Mechanism, how does it work?"

Brown sat upright. His eyes positively glowed with an inner light. "It is a highly secret European Union program to weaken the strongest economies until they are as poor as the poorest member states. The plan for convergence is no longer by strengthening the weaker member states until their economies are as strong as that of the UK. It is the reverse. The strongest economy will be brought crashing down. Their intention is to create a failure of the UK's economy requiring us to accept a financial bailout and the accompanying demand to adopt the Euro. The bailout will be on crippling repayment terms. Applying your earlier analogy, the eldest child will be forced to give its pocket money to the youngest. The means by which they will do it is the Athena Mechanism."

I was confused: "I still haven't quite understood. So how will they achieve that? How will the Athena Mechanism be implemented in practice?"

Brown visibly shivered despite the warmth given off by the Aga in the corner of the farmhouse kitchen. "By intentionally importing into this country's food supply half a ton of infected grass seed containing a virus powerful enough to create a nationwide pandemic…. *You* are the Athena Mechanism Mr Luttrell!"

CHAPTER 13

I realised that my mouth had fallen open and rubbed my face with my hands in an unconscious, futile attempt to wash all this away. I felt like pinching myself, but had no doubt that this wasn't a bad dream. I was becoming a tiny part in an international political conspiracy and there was nothing that I could do about it. "Well why is MI5 allowing this to happen? If the Government is aware of these plans, then why not arrest all those involved and confiscate the grass seed, destroy it, make sure it can never be used for such an evil purpose?"

Brown stiffened, his hands clasping the arms of his chair, his knuckles white. "The world has changed. Indeed, our Government's outlook has changed. We don't see the European Union as an existential threat, we see it as the way forward, the future. Unquestioning. We no longer think nationally, critically evaluating the real threats to this great nation. There is no black and white thinking anymore, every policy decision is nuanced and multi-faceted. The civil service no longer represent the UK, they represent the EU."

His face had become flushed. He swiped the air angrily with his hand before continuing. "They attend

workshops and training courses specifically inten-
tioned to change their viewpoint from a domestic one
to an international hotchpotch of globalisation, statism
and political correctness. To put one's national interest
ahead of the great project would be career suicide for
any politician or civil servant. Indeed, anyone showing
the critical faculties to even evaluate the real situation
is side-lined or demoted, ridiculed as being behind the
times and backward facing. Not PC. Our government
does not see itself as independent anymore, it isn't *about*
to cede national sovereignty to the European Union, it
already *has*. Fait accomplis. They just haven't told the
British people yet. It would be like turning *oneself* in to
the police. There is no dividing line between Brussels
and London."

I rubbed my eyes. "But that is incredible, are you
really telling me that the British security services have
identified a national threat but are simply unable to do
anything about it because our politicians have sold us
out?"

"It's not as simple as that Mr Luttrell. As I said,
it's more nuanced. An environment has been created
within Government and Whitehall in which it is quite
simply anathema to even consider or impute that the
European Union may be a threat to this nation. We are
not an independent country anymore, just a member
state whose people haven't accepted the propaganda,
haven't yet allowed themselves to be led down the same
pilgrim's path that their leaders have so willingly gal-
loped along. An island nation's resolve is not so easily
broken."

Brown quickly cleared the lump in his throat, before

continuing: "My team within MI5 is small and fairly autonomous. I have worked for the service for over 30 years, one of the most experienced operatives, and my team are treated accordingly. We are left alone. When we identified this threat, we sat on it and watched carefully what would develop. We had to. To report what we have discovered would have led to scorn, denial and ridicule. I may be in a position to retire, but my team are not. Their careers would be ruined. Posted overseas. Moved out of the way."

"So what are you telling me? That we just let these fanatical maniacs destroy our economy, because it is in the interests of the grand project? What are we supposed to do? Just lie back and take one for the team!? Cause the death and suffering of millions of animals and likely hundreds of thousands of human beings just because that is the way the world works? That's outrageous!"

Brown stood up and placed a kettle on the Aga in the corner of the kitchen. He leant against the hot stove, his thin frame soaking up the warmth. "I'm not suggesting that the situation is hopeless, no. What I am saying is that you won't find the Government, or Security Service, officially sanctioning the arrest of those employed by or serving the European Union to the detriment of this nation. The ensuing diplomatic crisis would be too unpalatable. However, I do believe that out of every threat comes an opportunity. An opportunity to break the grasp of the infernal European Union over this country. An opportunity to restore democracy and national sovereignty." He turned and poured us both a cup of tea.

Placing the cup and saucer in front of me on the table, he sat back down and continued. "When I first joined the Secret Service, we were taught that in order to ensure the security of this country, it was necessary to first understand its history. Political tensions and threats could only be understood - and, therefore, eliminated - if first placed in a historical context. Nowadays the new recruits are trained in esoteric concepts - thought leadership, neuro-linguistic programming, the importance of self not country, that kind of thing." He said witheringly.

"They are taught that there is no right or wrong, just shades of grey. Do what thou wilt. We seem to have forgotten that history informs the future. That only by learning from the past can we hope to understand the present and prepare for the future. The European Union is just another empire - created by treaty, bribery and incitement rather than outright violence, I grant you - but nonetheless just another empire that will eventually crumble just like those that have gone before it. Truly, there is nothing new under the sun."

Brown sipped from his cup, those bright eyes focused into the far distance, his face suddenly flushed again. "On the 22nd June 1940 the French surrendered to the Germans. The decisive German victory in the Battle of France left Britain's ally no choice but to capitulate. The Germans occupied northern and western France, controlling all of their Channel and Atlantic ports. If the Germans or Italians were able to go on to take control of the French naval fleet and combine it with their own then the balance of power at sea would swing strongly in Germany's favour. Our security as an island would be severely compromised. If our navy could not defend us then it looked as if Hitler's plan to invade Britain would be achieved successfully." He looked over at me: "Frightening times for a nation that must have felt it was making a stand against evil alone and unsupported."

"Winston Churchill was faced with the most difficult decision of his prime ministerial career. One that, most likely, haunted him for the rest of his life. He sought American help, but they wouldn't give it. Probably believing that it was a lost cause. He was given assurances from the French that they would never allow their naval fleet to fall into the hands of the Germans. Assurances from an occupied country that had surrendered without first notifying its allies, in breach of explicit treaty agreement. Were assurances enough when the outcome of the war and the freedom of the British people were at stake?"

Brown shrugged. "Churchill clearly didn't believe so. Black and white thinking was called for, not nuanced shades of grey. Churchill ordered the British Navy to commence Operation Catapult, intended to take the French ships out of the war. The British Navy tracked down the French warships and gave them an ultimatum containing three options - surrender their vessels to the British, destroy them or completely remove them from the theatre of war by sailing to the Caribbean or the United States. Many French commanders did just that and several ships were handed over to the British to continue the war effort."

"The French naval fleet was widely dispersed, but the most powerful concentration was at the port of Mers-el-Kebir in French Algeria. A British fleet surrounded the port and their Admiral was given six hours to accept the British ultimatum. He refused. He may have been upset that a mere Captain had been deputised to offer the ultimatum to him. The British Navy opened fire upon their ally's ships. Those ships were lying at anchor in a narrow port. 1,297 French sailors were killed and a further 350 were wounded." He shook his head. "It was a "turkey shoot", as our American cousins might say. The British killed more French in that one engagement than the Germans managed in any other engagement of the entire Second World War."

Brown's head drooped, but he slowly and determinedly lifted it before continuing.

"Sometimes the right decision is also the most terrible one. The hardest one to take. Many historians believed it changed the course of the war. They argue that it showed the Yanks our mettle and demonstrated that we British weren't going to capitulate. Ever. Within months the Americans had bolstered the allied fleet to the tune of 50 ships." He paused.

In shock, I said: "That is terrible, I can't imagine what it must have felt like to fire upon your own ally".

Brown turned again towards me. It was now dark outside and very dim in the kitchen, but I could see that his clear, blue eyes were glistening, filled with tears.

"You will Simon, you will."

I exploded: "What on earth do you mean by that?"

Brown approached the kitchen table until his face was merely inches away from my own. "I want you to deliver that contaminated seed to mainland France and then it will be distributed for use throughout France and Spain. We will see to that. The enemy believes that by *converging* the economies of the member states it will save the European Union. To ensure the reverse, we must ensure that those economies *diverge*."

"Spain already has one of the weakest, most problematic economies in the whole of the Eurozone. Nearly two in three Spaniards under the age of 25 do not have a job. Their austerity program succeeding only in compounding their economic deficit, not reducing it. A debt spiral. The social fabric is beginning to unravel." He shook his head.

"France's economy has been propped up thus far, but it is unsustainable too. It is heading for the same fate. We must further weaken their economies. Weaken them so substantially that a monetary union cannot possibly be maintained. A catastrophic pandemic of Foot and Mouth Virus will cause an economic collapse so considerable that they will urgently require a bail out from their European neighbours. The Germans, the British and the Scandinavians will baulk at the cost to them, to their taxpayers. There will be popular revolt and the European Union will be despised and revealed to be the doomsday machine that it truly is. The empire will crumble."

He collapsed into his seat, seemingly exhausted at the bringing to life of something that must have occupied his every waking moment since the contaminated seeds had first been stolen. I didn't say a word, my mind too absorbed with considering the enormity of what had just been proposed.

Brown made one final effort to pull himself upright and said: "There is one further thing that I must tell you.

It's a little closer to home than the evil machinations of a self-serving political elite. For the last ten days or so we have placed Officer Howe under surveillance. We have been watching and following him. I know, for example, that he came to your boatyard last night. To finalise the details of the shipment, I presume?" I nodded. "We have also placed him under electronic surveillance, with the help of a friend, another old timer like me still fighting the good fight, who works at GCHQ. Every email, text message, phone call made by Howe and his use of the web monitored and reported to me."

He looked sideways at me. "It may be of some little concern to you that Howe has spent the last three days establishing a false background for you and Miss Neilsen: Intelligence reports, web browsing history, intercepted communications. That sort of thing. All intended to identify you both as committed terrorists. Fanatical to the core. The powerful, nihilistic cell of the Occupy Movement determined to destroy capitalism......He plans to attribute the virus outbreak to you and Occupy by way of several false flags." He paused, toying with his wristwatch.

Brown's eyebrows arched upwards, creasing his forehead. "You didn't really expect that Howe would let you and Vilda just walk away, hand in hand, happily ever after into the sunset, did you?"

I didn't reply - he wasn't expecting me to.

"You are going to help me Simon, because you have no choice. I'm very sorry to have to put it to you that way, really I am".

My cheeks felt hot and my jaw involuntarily

clenched. I exploded: "I am fed up of being used. Fed up of being passed around like a crack pipe in a junkies' den. Just supposing that I do as you ask and divert the shipment of seed to you, for MI5 to distribute in France and Spain. How can I know that I won't be set up for that? Are you better or worse than the other lot? Why should I trust you?"

There was the briefest hint of a smile on Brown's face. The first that I had seen. His left hand reached into an inside jacket pocket and pulled out two passports which he slid along the table to me. I thumbed open the one on top. My picture, not my name. I looked in the other - a recent picture of Vilda, but not her name. Both German. He had a sense of humour at least.

"And the money in my Guernsey bank account? How do I know that won't be touched?" He pulled the final document out of his jacket pocket and slid it along the table. It was an account book for a Spanish bank, in the joint names of our newly created identities.

"You can transfer the money into this account tonight. I understand that you and Vilda hope to set up home in Mallorca. Very wise. I should keep away from mainland Spain if I was you. I understand that you can pick up some very funny bugs there."

CHAPTER 14

Luttrell was returned to the boatyard that evening. They took a quiet lane and dropped him on the edge of Salcombe, leaving him to walk the remaining two miles or so. It gave him an opportunity to try to get his head around what he had just been told and the arrangements that had been made. He was being used and there didn't seem to be a damn thing that could be done about it. He was a small part in a political power play, just a cog in a much larger machine. An innocent bystander dragged into a struggle by the machinations of a remote, self-serving political elite.

Brown, in his calm, supercilious way had instructed Luttrell to rendez-vous with the Border Force boat, as per the original plan. He was to take delivery of the contaminated seed and start his journey back to Salcombe. Clearly, he was going to be shadowed and watched by Howe's team every step of the way - from handover until the seed was successfully delivered to the warehouse. Any deviation from the agreed plan and Howe's team would intervene.

Brown had figured out a way to switch the seed during the trip back across the Channel. Unseen, his team would take the contaminated seed and leave Luttrell with a replacement cargo of untainted seed and allow him to continue his journey. The Border Force guys would be none the wiser and Brown's team could then use the contaminated seed in the way that he had suggested. As ever with politics and covert operations, the ends justified the means. MI5 were prepared to implement the optimum solution, even where the collateral damage would be horrendous. Mers-el-Kebir.

Luttrell slowly opened his eyes. The fresh sheet on his bed had been creased while he tossed and turned and looked as if it had been slept on, unchanged, for weeks. Sleep was the one thing that he hadn't got. A full ashtray on the floor, to the side of the bed. He rose and flicked a switch - the electronic blinds on the skylights retracting to reveal a beautiful clear blue sky. An area of high pressure had settled in and it looked like the weather was set fair for his crossing that afternoon to Guernsey. He picked up his iPad from the coffee table and checked the tide times. Good, he would be leaving just as high tide had flowed to the highest point in the estuary. A light wind and good visibility had been predicted. Perfect conditions for crossing the Channel.

He walked naked into the bathroom and splashed warm water on his face. He picked up his razor and regarded himself in the mirror. He placed the razor down without shaving, but continued to look into his own eyes for some considerable time. He stepped into the shower, turned the shower control to cold and held himself under the icy rivulets until he could stand it no more. He dressed and sauntered downstairs to the boat showroom clasping a steaming mug of coffee. He opened up the showroom and switched on the radio - it was tuned to Classic FM. He smiled to himself. Steve and Andy's little joke, no doubt. They should be turning up for work in five minutes or so and he booted up the computer on the sales desk, pleased to return to the mundane work of the boatyard after the high drama of the last couple of days.

Steve arrived first, his breakfast croissant half eaten in his large hand. He saw Luttrell at the computer. "Excuse me, who are you? How did you get in here?" Luttrell lifted his hand to bat away the banter. "When you own the place you can take as many days off as you like. Anyway, from what I can see on this computer you have only sold one boat in the whole week I have been away. Did the front door get stuck?" Steve sat down at the desk and shot out his hand to try to grab the boss's coffee. It was moved before he even got close and he received a less than playful club around the ear for his cheek.

Luttrell perched on the edge of his desk. "I need you to do something for me Steve. I am taking the RIB over to Guernsey to see Vilda this afternoon." Steve smirked: "Can I come boss?" Luttrell laughed: "Funny you should say that, but I do need you to sail over to Guernsey in Peregrine". Peregrine was Luttrell's yacht, which he moored on a buoy in the estuary. "Vilda and I are going to take a week out sailing. The forecast is good and we are going to have a leisurely sail along the northern French coast. Can you provision her for a week's sailing, fill her up with fuel and check the battery level? Make sure that her water tanks are filled too".

Luttrell shifted uneasily on the desk. "I need to get

over there today for a meeting, so I'll take the RIB and leave about 3pm. I expect that I will pass you on the way. If you leave early enough, you might get over there while it is still light." Steve nodded. "I have called the marina at St. Peter Port and it is full, so why don't you anchor her in a bay and spend the night on her? I'll call you in the morning and Vilda and I will come and find you. There is a beer in it for you. Do you think you can manage that?"

Steve smiled: "Aye, aye skipper". Luttrell opened the desk draw and gave him a wad of notes. "Remember, a week's worth of food and check her over carefully. I'll need two sets of rough weather gear on board too, just in case the weather turns."

As Steve left the boatyard, he crossed in the doorway with his fellow employee Andy. Luttrell picked up a white, sailing cap that was lying around the boatyard and placed it on Andy's head. "Andy, looks like you are going to be in charge of the boatyard for a couple of days. I am going to be away for at least a week. See if you can sell more than one boat while I am away this time?" Andy smiled, "that will depend on whether the Surf's up, bro!"

Luttrell spent the rest of the morning at the computer checking the tide, weather and wind for the Channel Islands and northern France. He also logged on to the website of his Guernsey bank and transferred the entire amount to the Spanish bank account details that Brown had given him. No turning back now. He went up to the sail loft and called Vilda. He couldn't tell her why, but he needed her to be ready.

At lunchtime Luttrell sauntered down to the chandlcry shop on Island Street. It was a yachtie's paradise, every inch of the store filled with sailing equipment and marine clothing. He purchased 30 metres of heavy duty monofilament nylon line. The type used by fishermen to make drift nets. It was clear in colour and would float on the surface, virtually indestructible. He also purchased a box of emergency flares, a diving knife, a five litre jerry can and a four man Crewsaver liferaft packed into a holdall but which automatically self-inflated on deployment into the water. He returned to the boatyard and stowed his purchases in the RIB, first filling the jerry can with petrol from a larger container that he kept in a store room at the boatyard. He put on his life vest over his sailing jacket and fastened the kill-chord around his right thigh. He checked his pockets for the passports, his mobile phone and wallet. Sunglasses on. He was all set.

Luttrell manoeuvred the RIB slowly away from the pontoon and headed seaward down the estuary. He had left just before high tide, when the water in the estuary was slack. The RIB's bow effortlessly carved through the calm water and he let the boat ease up onto the plane, the helm becoming alive and sharp in his hands. He ignored the speed limit and the Harbour Master's shaken fist, he didn't plan on returning any time soon.

He passed over the bar at mouth of the estuary and buried the throttles, setting a course for Guernsey. The roar of the twin diesel engines echoing back from the cliffs, at odds with the calm sea and conditions. Gulls and terns wheeled overhead and he looked back at the coastline in the sunshine. He got the feeling that he might not see the estuary, the cliffs, or the rocky outcrops ever again. So be it, Mallorca had considerable charms of its own. No looking back.

He scanned the horizon for other vessels. There were no recreational sailors out, the wind was too light for a meaningful sail but he could make out the outline of a large cargo ship in the far distance. The Channel is the world's busiest seaway, with over 500 commercial vessels passing through each day. The speed and size of these behemoths has to be seen to be believed. A cargo ship or passenger ferry that was first glimpsed many miles away could be upon you seemingly in the blink of an eye. They wouldn't, or couldn't, deviate from their course no matter what recreational traffic was crossing the shipping lane. They followed a very precise automated course, often one ship directly behind the other, and this together with the momentum that they carried and the massive fuel impact of slowing from their optimum cruise speed meant that any recreational sailor wishing to cross a shipping lane took great care to keep out of their way.

Luttrell's RIB had a comprehensive GPS navigation system with a ship tracker app that plotted the path and speed of these mighty vessels and, in real time, showed that information relative to the course that the RIB was taking, sounding an alarm if it appeared that a collision course was being maintained. The sheer speed of the RIB meant that Luttrell was confident of its ability to keep him out of any trouble when sailing by line of sight through the busiest shipping channel, but an experienced sailor always relied on his instruments and Luttrell duly checked his course on the map plotter. Plenty of traffic, but no problems. He cleared the shipping lane and headed east towards Guernsey.

He relaxed his grip on the helm, switching on the autopilot, and pulled a pair of binoculars out of the locker in the console. He should be catching up with Steve on Peregrine any time soon - like a racing car chasing down a horse drawn cart. The visibility was excellent and Luttrell soon picked out a likely looking mast. He shut off the autopilot and steered towards it. As he approached Peregrine he could see that the mainsail was up, despite the lack of wind. Luttrell guessed that Steve had raised the sail to be more easily seen as he crossed over the shipping lane and because it helped to steady the boat in the light swell as she motored along.

Luttrell admired her lines as he approached. Najad were a Swedish manufacturer of elegant but seaworthy yachts, popular with "blue water" cruisers and others who valued good sea keeping and excellent build quality. A yacht to cross oceans in, she would make light work of this Channel crossing. Steve was standing at one of her twin wheels and as Luttrell came closer still he could see a can of beer in his hand. He picked up his speed to 50 knots and speared past the yacht, only metres from the hull. Rooster tails of water thrown up by the twin props soaking one side of the yacht as he did so. Steve dropped his beer and Luttrell laughed, picking up the radio. He and Steve always used the same radio channel when out boating, ignoring proper operating procedure which required users to establish contact on Channel 16 before switching to a less busy channel.

Luttrell tuned the dial to Channel 78 and he quickly

got through. "Terribly sorry that you spilt your beer mate, expect that you have plenty more down below!" Steve laughed and said "I forget just how fast that RIB is! What a day for a sail. I must call Andy at the boatyard and let him know what he is missing."

Luttrell replied: "Tell him that I think he's a star for holding the fort for me. I'll catch up with you in the morning. Don't drink too much beer!" Luttrell turned and waved, replacing the handset before continuing on with his journey.

Less than an hour later he was approaching St Peter Port. He throttled back and piloted the RIB through the gap in the sea wall into the marina. He shook out his legs. They had taken the brunt of the pounding from the high speed crossing and the muscles in his thighs and calves were tired. He radioed the Harbour Master and asked if there was a free berth he could use overnight. Contrary to what he had told Steve earlier in the day, there were plenty of berths and he soon had the RIB secured against a pontoon. He left the engines idling for a couple of minutes, so that they could cool, before killing the ignition. He needed a coffee and a cigarette and pulled out his phone to call Vilda as he made his way on foot out of the marina.

...

A lone man, overweight and balding, wearing a grey hooded top and sunglasses, sipping coffee and reading a yachting magazine on the terrace of a café, observed his arrival. The man picked up his phone, punched in some digits, and announced "Luttrell is here. No… by himself. He has just walked out of the marina and is heading along the seafront. I'll keep you informed." He drained the last mouthful of coffee, threw some coins on the table and followed.

CHAPTER 15

As Luttrell walked along the quay in the early evening sunshine, he couldn't help but be struck by the irony. Tomorrow this beautiful and serene place was going to be the starting point for a chain of events that would lead to a pandemic virus being unleashed in continental Europe. One that would destroy the food production capabilities of France and Spain, in turn crippling their already weakened economies. It would probably lead to such devastation that riot and disorder on a scale not seen in the Western world in modern times were bound to follow. He shuddered inwardly, in shock as to what was about to unfold.

Brown had a truly brilliant yet malevolent mind to think of it. To turn a European Union threat to the economic livelihood and social stability of the UK back on itself in such a way that two of the largest economies in the Eurozone would falter and stumble, crashing the aggressor itself onto the rocks, was near perfect irony but cruel too. The Athena Mechanism hoisted by its own petard.

This wasn't just some socio-economic power play created by an out of touch political elite. There would be a real human cost - a devastating one. Food riots, civil unrest, a loss of faith in the ability of governments to govern. There would be real tragedy and suffering. Luttrell reflected on the history lesson he had received from Brown on the sinking of allied ships at Mers-el-Kebir and Churchill's belief that, where national security was concerned, the end *always* justified the means. Collateral damage was a factor to be disregarded, not relevant to the central issue. The optimum solution was the optimum solution. Leaders had to see clearly, to be dispassionate. No shades of grey.

And yet….. It seemed to Luttrell that the present circumstances were somehow different. Society and human behaviour was different now to how they had been in the early days of World War 2. The horrors of war and the brutal slaughter it entailed surely could no longer be countenanced in the age of total knowledge? The speed of communications and the total flood of comprehensive information by virtue of the internet meant that the stark reality of any conflict, disorder or suffering would be transmitted in minute, terrible detail to every computer, smartphone, television or radio.

Luttrell couldn't be a part of it. There had to be another way....

Vilda threw her arms around him and kissed him passionately on the lips. He had been so engrossed in thought that he had been totally oblivious to his surroundings. Her soft, moist lips and welcoming body were at odds with their goodbye at the airport just a few days ago. "Whoa there! Take it easy, my lip is damaged. A crazy girl tried to bite it hard enough to draw blood!"

Vilda laughed "You are the crazy one! We get caught

for smuggling cigarettes and the very next thing you want to do is smuggle more! You don't learn from your mistakes, do you?" "Clearly not, I am still in love with you aren't I?" She dug him playfully in the ribs with her elbow. Luttrell placed his arm around her shoulder, turned her around and marched her along the road. "Come on, there are some things I need you to do for me tomorrow, let's talk it through at your hotel. You might also have to grant a condemned man his last wish!"

. . .

They walked into the lobby of her hotel. Twenty metres back the man in the grey hooded top, who had followed them along the quay from a discreet distance, pulled his mobile phone out of his pocket. "Luttrell and his girlfriend have just entered her hotel....No, no reason to be worried. No, everything looks fine. I'll wait here in case they go anywhere else this evening. I will let you know if they move on".

. . .

Vilda used her key card to let them into the sparse, but not unwelcoming hotel room, common to any hotel chain the world over. It was saved from being totally non-descript by French windows leading out to a small balcony which overlooked the port, bathed in the weak evening sunshine. Luttrell drew the curtains, closing out the beautiful view and reducing the room to near darkness. He kicked off his deck shoes, reclined on the bed and switched on a table lamp. He motioned for Vilda to join him. "In a minute I want you to go down to reception and extend your reservation for the rest of this week. Order some food to be sent up to the room while you are down there. If anyone is in the reception area, speak loudly and make sure that you are overheard. Have a bottle of wine sent up too."

Vilda nodded but looked puzzled. "Why do we need the room for the rest of the week? Are you coming back here once you have delivered the cigarettes to the warehouse?"

Luttrell shook his head, his brow furrowed. "I need to ask you to do something." He put his hand up to quell the inevitable question that he could see forming on her beautiful lips. "I am not going to make the final delivery tomorrow. I am going to pick up the cigarettes from Edouard in the morning but not complete the journey back to the UK. I can't tell you how or why, but I need your help. You will have to trust me." He smiled. "Think of it as training for when we live together!"

He ducked the thrown pillow and watched as Vilda let herself out of the hotel room door. Once she had sorted out their reservation and food he would outline to her what she and Steve needed to do with Peregrine in the morning. It would make no sense to her, but he knew she would and could do it - he was confident of that. He just wished that he was as confident about what he must do tomorrow.

...

Steve lowered the main sail and furled it carefully home between the lazy jacks, securely stowed against the boom. The light wind had dropped to an almost perfect calm, the last rays of sunshine were highlighting the sandy beach of La Fontenelle, on the north shore of Guernsey. The yacht's radio, still tuned to Channel 78, was silent.

Peregrine was at anchor a hundred metres or so off the beach and, while drinking yet another can of beer, Steve sat for a moment checking that the anchor had held. He created a sight line by lining up an old World War Two gun turret that lay just beyond the beach, with a rocky outcrop and monitored the boat's position for a while. Satisfied that Peregrine wasn't dragging, he cracked open another beer and settled in for the night. There were no other boats in the bay and he would have a peaceful night, the gentle motion of the boat more soporific than an old rocking chair.

CHAPTER 16

Luttrell woke early. Vilda was still fast asleep, her head resting against his chest, her long blonde hair cascading across his shoulder and along the pillow. Unusually, they had slept the whole night in each other's arms, notwithstanding the warmth of the duvet and the slightly stuffy hotel room. It was a long time since they had done that, but she was concerned at what lay ahead - worse for her as Luttrell had not been able to tell her why he needed her and Steve to sail Peregrine to a rendez-vous point half way across the Channel this very morning and wait for him to make contact with them on the yacht's radio.

He had handed her the two false passports and the bank book for the Spanish bank account, in a water-proof grab bag. He had told her that if he hadn't made contact by 1pm then she and Steve must sail on to Salcombe without him. She hadn't asked why he might not make contact. She had figured that out for herself.

Luttrell stared at the ceiling of the hotel room for some time, running through the steps he planned to take over and over in his head until he was satisfied that he had covered every angle and anticipated every possible eventuality. He gently eased her head off his chest and on to the pillow. He kissed her lightly on the lips and, reluctantly, climbed out of bed and walked into the bathroom. He quickly shaved and showered, hardly conscious of his surroundings.

Vilda was awake and nearly fully dressed when he re-entered the bedroom. Silently they packed all of their things in to Luttrell's holdall. Vilda was to leave the hotel fifteen minutes after Luttrell left for the marina. She was to take a taxi to La Fontenelle beach and, with the grab bag, swim out to Peregrine. She was to tell Steve that they needed to leave immediately and set sail for the pre-arranged rendez-vous point mid-Channel.

Luttrell walked out of the hotel and turned left along the quay towards the marina. He called in to the Harbour Master's office and paid the tariff for the overnight berth. He walked along the pontoon and threw the holdall into the RIB, fired-up her engines and released the mooring lines. As he headed off to the fuel berth, he didn't look back. If he had, he would have seen a fat man in a grey hooded top sitting and enjoying a coffee at a pavement café while talking into his mobile phone. Luttrell already knew that every step he would take today would be monitored and reported to Howe. The slightest apparent deviation to the plan agreed with Howe and their deal would be off. Howe had told him as much in no uncertain terms.

Luttrell guessed that Brown's men would also be watching him, perhaps even watching Howe's men too. It wasn't going to be easy, but today he would outfox them both and sail off into the sunset. His plan had to work. Good always won out over evil, didn't it?

CHAPTER 17

The fuel barge was busy, two yachts were tied alongside occupying the only fuel rig. Luttrell circled the port, the twin engines barely ticking over, while he waited for them to refuel. No matter. It was only 9.15 and he had plenty of time before he was due to meet Edouard at 10am.

One of the yachts moved away from the barge and he gently brought the big RIB alongside, directing the attendant to fill her up. It took five minutes or so to fill the large under deck fuel tank and Luttrell paid the attendant, attached the kill-chord to his thigh and put on his life vest. There was a wind picking up from the south-west and he zipped up his yachting jacket and cast a look at the overcast, threatening sky. He guessed that it would rain later and hoped that it would hold off just long enough for him to do what needed to be done.

The attendant untied his mooring line and Luttrell slowly manoeuvred the RIB away from the fuel barge and gently eased the throttles open as he headed out of St Peter Port. The tide was running against him as he motored south towards Sark and he pushed the twin throttle levers hard open, eager to get on with it.

The last few days had been taken up with preparation for today and concern over what was to come. Being told what to do. He finally felt in control and in his element, confident and even excited about what he now had to carry out. He remembered this feeling from missions undertaken with the Marines. The planning stage was always the worst, anticipation worse than the real thing. Once the mission started he always felt supremely confident and in control. The nerves and stress disappeared.

The big RIB crashed through an oncoming wave, spray left trailing either side of the hull as the boat momentarily jumped clear of the water before landing back on top of the next wave crest, powering on. He smiled to himself. He might even enjoy it.

As the boat passed along the west coast of Sark he looked around to see if he could identify the vessel that Howe's team would use. There were a few yachts making the most of today's stronger wind, but he couldn't see any kind of Border Force vessel. He guessed that they would be on the other side of the island - a better vantage point to oversee Edouard's delivery of the cigarettes and to then shadow him to the meeting point on the east coast of Herm, where it had been agreed he would pick up the contaminated grass seed.

Luttrell throttled back a little, engaged the auto pilot and checked the items in the stern locker that he had purchased from the chandlers. He rearranged them so that the flares and jerry can were together at the bottom of the locker - inwardly smiling at what he would have said to Steve or Andy if they had ever stored those items together in a boat locker. He placed the holstered diving knife in the cargo pocket of his trousers, placed the liferaft handles facing upwards and finally placed the monofilament nylon fishing line at the very top, casting an eye over it to ensure it wasn't snagged and that it would readily deploy. He closed the locker and returned to the helm, deactivating the auto pilot function on the GPS.

He was nearing the southerly point of Sark and he altered course to follow the coastline towards Dixcart Bay. He could see that Edouard was already anchored in the bay and headed over to him. He noticed a large, grey RIB a mile or so beyond Edouard's boat. It looked to be a similar size to his own boat, but with a crew of 4 on board and two large outboard motors. He couldn't be sure at this distance, but he guessed that it was a Zodiac Hurricane - tough, professional boats much favoured by Special Forces and military applications worldwide. Those two huge outboards would give it a turn of speed too.

In other circumstances he would have relished pitting his RIB-X against it, but he hoped that wouldn't be necessary today.

"Ca va Edouard?" He was alongside Edouard's fishing boat and they quickly secured the two boats together. Edouard was wearing a set of yellow waterproofs and grumbled: "Oui, yes, all fine, I suppose. I think we will have some rain today and I haven't caught a thing in two days. If this keeps up I am going to have to ask you for more money for the cigarettes!"

Luttrell looked at the fisherman's tanned, heavily lined and inscrutable face. He wondered if Edouard had been "got at" by Howe's team and if he was one of the one's who were prepared to make false testimony against him? He hoped that he would never know.

"Go on with you Edouard, you will probably have your best catch ever today. You might even hook a beautiful mermaid and give your wife something to be jealous about!" Edouard smiled and shook his head.

Luttrell clapped his hands. "Come on old man, let's get those cigarettes on board and I will leave you to catch those fish." Luttrell filled up the RIB's lockers with the cigarette cartons and handed Edouard his payment in Euros. They untied the lines uniting the two boats and Luttrell headed off in the direction from which he had come, as he had agreed with Howe.

He turned and waved to Edouard and looked beyond him to the big grey Zodiac - it was turning and looked to be headed northwards. It must be Howe's team. They would run around the island in the opposite direction to him and Luttrell calculated that they should arrive at the meeting point on Herm having covered approximately the same distance. So far, so good.

Luttrell was now heading in the same direction as the tide and the wind. The wind flattened the wave chop that he had faced on the way to Sark and the tide's movement gave him a few more knots of speed over the ground. It might be useful to find out the relative performances of the two boats and he pushed both throttles fully open. The bespoke racing diesel engines roared and flung the RIB forward. The hull, stepped in two places, was a very low drag design and he quickly reached an indicated speed of 75 miles per hour.

It was only 5 miles to the rendez-vous point with

Howe's team and Luttrell was at full throttle for what seemed like only moments before having to ease back as he approached the bay of Shell Beach on the east coast of Herm. He was pleased to note that the grey Zodiac hadn't reached the bay yet. He turned and saw it some mile away still, but closing rapidly. He couldn't be sure how hard they had been pushing the Zodiac, but being ahead of them reassured him and strengthened his belief that his was the faster boat.

He headed for the middle of the bay and then motored slowly towards the shore until he could see through the clear water that he was in a depth of around ten metres. He walked forward and lowered the anchor. As he did so he looked towards the beach. Howe had picked this spot well. It was very remote and they would not be seen by anyone. He turned towards the noise of the approaching Zodiac.

The four crew, all male, were wearing grey uniforms which displayed no insignia or identification whatsoever. They wore helmets and the obligatory sunglasses, despite the overcast day. As they circled his boat a couple of times, Luttrell noticed that the two outboards were 175 horsepower each. Tremendously powerful, but even their combined force would still give this sturdy, heavily built craft considerably poorer performance than his own. There were no identifying marks on the vessel at all, but Luttrell could see five red crates lashed to the deck in the middle of the boat.

They had not attempted to make any communication whatsoever with him so far, not even eye contact. The crew member at the helm took a mobile phone from his grey jacket and began a conversation. Luttrell could not hear what was being said, their boat was still 50 metres or so away and he was downwind of them. He guessed that they were seeking clearance from Howe to proceed with the handover. This was evidently received, for they soon turned and motored very slowly towards him.

Luttrell's boat was swinging on its anchor, moving slightly as a result of the wind and tide. Nonetheless, their helmsman expertly brought the Zodiac alongside with only the lightest of impacts, their bow pointing in the opposite direction to his own. The crew attached two lines to secure the boats together, requiring neither assistance nor permission. "Good morning" Luttrell ventured. The man at the helm nodded, almost imperceptibly, and replied: "Are you Simon Luttrell?" The English was heavily accented, he guessed possibly Dutch.

"I am. Officer Howe told me to meet you here and take that consignment from you for.....onward transmission". He was gesturing at the red crates lashed to the deck of the Zodiac.

The skipper nodded again and turned to his crew. "Pass the crates over and see that they are safely stowed."

Luttrell was expecting the crew to pass him the crates, but one of the crew leapt over the tubing into the RIB-X and turned to receive the shipment from his colleagues. His forearms, revealed by his grey, short sleeved shirt, were well muscled and entirely tattooed from elbow to wrist, both arms. The remaining two crew members passed over the crates and the tattooed man fastened them off against the rear bulkhead with cordage passed over to him from the Zodiac, before re-joining his boat. He had handled the 50 kg crates of seed as if they were empty, notwithstanding the rolling motion of the two boats.

The Zodiac's skipper untied the kill-chord from his thigh and clambered over the tubes onto Luttrell's boat. He checked that the crates had been securely stowed, before turning to Luttrell. "You are to proceed exactly in accordance with the directions given to you by Officer Howe. We are instructed to observe your passage to Salcombe. We will maintain a discreet distance from you, but any deviation from the planned route, anything unexpected and we will intercept you and reclaim the shipment. You will be arrested and the consequences to you and your girlfriend will be as described to you by Officer Howe. Is that understood?"

Luttrell nodded. The skipper turned and stepped over the tubing back into the Zodiac. Two of the crew untied the mooring lines and the Zodiac turned and withdrew quickly, before easing back and standing off some two hundred metres from Luttrell's boat.

Luttrell turned his gaze from the Zodiac to the crates tied off against the rear bulkhead of his boat. They were red, sturdy plastic crates with a folding lid and secured in a way that allowed him to lift the lid of one of the topmost crates. It contained 5 unmarked cellophane wrapped packages, each the size of a kerbstone. He closed the lid, covered the crates with a tarpaulin, before checking his watch. He walked quickly to the bow of the boat and recovered the anchor. He had left the engines running throughout and turned the boat away from the beach, accelerating smoothly but rapidly to a 30 knot cruise.

Once clear of the bay he changed direction again, setting a course for Salcombe on his GPS. Over his shoulder he noticed that the Zodiac had not yet started to move. It was only when he was around a mile away from them that they began to follow him.

It would be tight, but at that distance he felt his plans could work. The rain that he had feared earlier was holding off and the sea conditions were calm. His confidence grew. He stood four-square at the helm of his boat as it powered through the slight chop, unflinching as spray from time to time whipped cold across his determined face.

CHAPTER 18

A further RIB was moving fast in the Channel that morning. It was black in colour, with seating for four and was propelled by a large outboard - the engine cover stripped of any branding and covered in non-reflective black paint. A sturdy, metal "A" Frame at the stern of the boat carried GPS and Communications equipment. Williams and Smith, the MI5 men who had forcefully brought Luttrell to the Devon farmhouse at Brown's request, occupied a bench seat and directly in front of which was a large, marine GPS chartplotter screen. A member of the Special Boat Service, who they had called upon to assist, steered the boat. Notwithstanding the military appearance of the vessel, they were dressed in civilian clothes - non-descript, sailing attire.

They had started their journey from Weymouth on England's south coast at 10 am and had proceeded due south across The Channel for 15 miles until they had reached the edge of the commercial shipping lane. There they waited as enormous cargo ships and tankers plied the shipping lane from east to west along The Channel, half a mile or so from where they were now slowly circling.

The software on their navigation computer allowed them to identify the cargo vessels moving along the shipping lane before they had even come into view. They were looking out for the Emma Maersk - capable of carrying a 154,000 ton cargo and at 397 metres long one of the largest cargo liners to use this shipping lane. She ran on a fixed schedule, published by the shipping company that owned her, which had allowed the MI5 team - and Brown in particular - to form their plans around her. She would shortly be passing along The Channel shipping lane en route from Rotterdam to Singapore.

As the team watched the screen a green blip appeared on the left hand edge, signifying the presence of the Emma Maersk. She would be with them in less than 5 minutes. The Brown plan was for the MI5 boat to shadow the Emma Maersk all of the way along the shipping lane, sticking as close as they dared to the mighty vessel's steel hull, and use her as a screen to deliver them to the point at which Luttrell's RIB would be crossing the shipping lane. They would be completely invisible to any vessel to the South of the shipping lane.

Luttrell had been instructed to cross the shipping lane directly in front of the path of the Emma Maersk, as close as he dared or his seamanship would allow. Once her hull shielded them from the prying eyes aboard Howe's team's Zodiac, Luttrell and the MI5 boat would reconnoitre unseen and transfer the contaminated seed from Luttrell's boat, replacing it with a normal crop. Luttrell would then continue with his journey, while the MI5 boat would travel hidden alongside the Emma Maersk until they were well out of sight.

At a normal economical cruising speed of 24 knots, the hull of the Emma Maersk would shield them from the view of the following Zodiac for around 30 seconds, perhaps longer if they could swap the containers of seed while their vessels were still moving. They were working on a timescale of around three seconds for each crate to be handed over from Luttrell's boat to the MI5 boat and a replacement crate handed back. An unsteady, continually moving marine environment subject to current, wind and the wash caused by a four hundred metre hull moving at 24 knots. No margin for error.

The MI5 guys had practiced this manoeuvre endlessly since Brown had formed his plan. It could be done and it would be done. The success or failure of the whole mission - so confidential that Brown had required his men not to disclose it to anyone, even fellow MI5 officers - depended on it.

The green blip grew closer on their chartplotter screen until the Emma Maersk hove into view, travelling fast towards them. She was in a convoy of cargo liners, a tanker in front and a cargo ship to the rear with only 500 metres at most separating them. The helmsman turned the black RIB into the shipping lane and then onto a parallel course, moving slowly ahead at a steady ten knots.

Within minutes the enormous hull of the Emma Maersk was alongside them. The noise of her single diesel engine - the world's largest single diesel unit and generating over 100,000 horsepower - was like the sound of thunder, but from directly inside the thunder cloud itself. The MI5 helmsman fought the huge wash and turbulence as the Emma Maersk's bulbous bow passed by them barely metres away.

He manoeuvred the black RIB into a spot alongside her about a third of the way along her hull where hydronamics caused a relatively calm area of water, so close into her hull that they were invisible to the merchant seamen on-board. The helmsman maintained this position, exactly matching the speed of the Emma Maersk, while Williams and Smith prepared for the critical liaison with Luttrell, only minutes away.

...

Vilda and Steve closely monitored the radio on-board Peregrine as they sailed away from Guernsey. Steve had been surprised, but not entirely disappointed, to see a dripping wet Vilda haul herself up the yacht's bathing ladder while he was still anchored in Guernsey's La Fontenelle bay. He hadn't exactly rushed to get her a towel and some dry clothes, much to Vilda's annoyance.

They had immediately shipped the anchor and set full sail on a course that had seen them cross over the shipping lane a couple of miles to the south west, as Vilda had been instructed by Luttrell on a hurried radio transmission that he had made after picking up the contaminated seed from the Zodiac RIB. Although they were in the much slower boat, they had the advantage over Luttrell of not having had the two rendez-vous to make, nor the accompanying detours to Sark and Herm, and so had crossed the shipping lane well ahead of Luttrell.

Once through the shipping lane they had hove-to with their sails flapping ineffectively in the wind, holding position mid-Channel. Luttrell had told them to wait for him there – he would come to them. If he hadn't joined them by 1pm then they were to sail on to Salcombe without him, Luttrell's plan having failed.

Vilda anxiously paced the deck of the yacht, from time to time viewing the horizon with a pair of binoculars. Steve settled back and cracked open a beer.

...

Luttrell maintained a steady course on his RIB. Some mile or so behind him was the Zodiac of Howe's team. They were close enough to keep him under effective surveillance, but far enough away so that any casual onlooker would not assume that they were travelling together or were in any way connected. Luttrell checked his watch and then scrolled through the screens on his chartplotter until he found the ship tracker application screen. He was around 3 miles from the beginning of the shipping lane and he guessed that the larger ship, far off to his right in the distance, and travelling in a tight convoy with several other cargo vessels would be the Emma Maersk. By hovering the cursor over the moving icons on his screen, it was possible to identify the names of the ships. It was the Emma Maersk and he slowed the RIB's pace slightly until a warning beep from the chartplotter informed him that he was now on a collision course with her.

He was supposed to wait until the cargo vessel was right on top of him before accelerating hard to cross her path just in front of her enormous, bulbous bow. There he could liaise with the MI5 boat, unseen by Howe's men. By the time he again became visible to them, he would have already switched the contaminated cargo for a clean one and resumed his expected course to Salcombe.

The MI5 boat would continue using the Emma Maersk as a moving shield until well out of the visible range of Howe's team in the Zodiac. Luttrell presumed that they would then set a course to mainland France in order to deliver the contaminated seed to continental Europe, in accordance with Brown's monstrous but brilliant plan to reverse the Athena Mechanism.

Luttrell was determined to prevent it happening. He pushed the two throttle levers hard against the throttle-stops and the boat leapt forward, the twin engines producing a deafening roar. He turned the helm to avoid crossing the path of the convoy of cargo vessels and accelerated along their line until he was just level with the protruding bulb shaped bow of the lead vessel – a fuel tanker. The hull of the tanker towered above his RIB like a cliff and the bow wave it was forming was fully two metres of foaming, breaking, white water. Luttrell intended to aim his RIB right at it and yanked hard on the steering wheel, pulling his RIB into and over the path of the big tanker by jumping off the two metre wall of water being pushed in front of its bow. His boat landed with a crash, but he had done it!

He had successfully passed in front of the tanker and was now in calmer water the other side of the tanker's hull - hidden from the view of Howe's team. He was also two miles ahead of the MI5 boat which couldn't leave the shadow of the Emma Maersk's hull without being seen. He had brought himself some time, but not much.

Luttrell brought the RIB to a shuddering halt by throwing the engines into reverse. He ran to the back of the boat and threw open the stern locker, grabbing the packaged liferaft and throwing it over the side into the sea. There was a loud bang as the self-inflation device was triggered and the in-built oxygen tank started to hiss as it quickly inflated the liferaft.

Luttrell used the diving knife to slash the ropes restraining the plastic crates against the rear bulkhead. Although around 50 kilograms in weight each, the adrenalin coursing around his body meant that he hardly noticed the weight at all as he threw all ten crates and the evil seed that they contained into the inflated liferaft. He leant deep into the stern locker and straightened up with the jerry can in his hand. The safety mechanism on the cap briefly delayed him opening it and he cursed his fumbling fingers, but within seconds he was dousing the seed packets and crates within the lifeboat with petrol. He threw the now empty can in there too and cut through the halyard still attaching the liferaft to his RIB. The liferaft was pulled away by the wash of the next cargo ship and, within seconds, was floating a good distance away.

Luttrell looked up to see how far away the MI5 RIB was. It was less than half a mile away, still shadowing the Emma Maersk, and they would be on him in seconds. He pulled a flare out of the locker and with one swift movement struck the base of it against the bulkhead and aimed it at the liferaft. A burning ball of white phosphorescence rocketed into the liferaft and it exploded with such intense heat that Luttrell could feel it burn against his cheeks even though it was some 30 metres away. The liferaft was totally engulfed in flames before sinking slowly beneath the surface.

He looked up to see that the MI5 boat was now only one hundred metres away and accelerating towards him. Luttrell retrieved the last item from the boat's locker. He paid out the nylon heavy duty monofilament fishing line over the stern of his boat, spreading it as wide as he possibly could. All 30 metres of the transparent but strong fishing line slipped into the water and began to splay out a little distance behind his boat. He waited until the MI5 RIB was only metres away from him before he ran to his own helm, slamming open the throttles.

As Luttrell's RIB accelerated away he looked over his shoulder for the MI5 boat – it had come to a standstill, the monofilament fishing line had fouled its propeller and disabled the boat completely.

Luttrell momentarily smiled to himself as adjusted his course and continued at top speed towards his rendez-vous point with Vilda and Steve on Peregrine. He checked the chart plotter and estimated that they were a little over five miles away from him. He presumed that they were blissfully unaware of the carnage that he had just caused.

As he cleared the convoy of cargo ships still travelling along the shipping lane, he looked back to spot the Zodiac of Howe's team. They were circling in a wide arc on the far side of the shipping lane, a mile or so behind. He guessed that they had seen the smoke sent up by the exploding liferaft and were in a quandary as to whether to investigate the cause of that or to give chase to him. They probably needed to call Howe for instructions. He smiled.

Their confusion gave him the breathing space that he needed and he pressed on, the hull of his RIB pounding the waves into submission as he flew over the surface of the water at top speed. As he did so, the rain that had been threatening to fall all day finally started to come down, reducing the visibility to a few hundred yards. He had got clean away.

Exhilaration and relief washed over him. Within seconds he was soaked to the skin, but there was a broad grin on his handsome, weather beaten face.

Using the chart plotter he came up on Peregrine floating motionless at the rendez-vous point. Steve and Vilda nowhere to be seen on deck, sheltering from the rain down below. As he pulled the RIB alongside the yacht he heard the hatch pull back and Vilda ran out to meet him. He stepped aboard and she flew into his arms. They kissed, oblivious to the pouring rain.

He looked over Vilda's shoulder to see Steve standing on deck, awkwardly shuffling from foot to foot and swigging from the ever present can of beer. Luttrell threw the RIB's keys to him: "Steve, take the RIB back home to Salcombe. Vilda and I have a little sailing trip planned….."

CHAPTER 19

There was no time to wave Steve off. Although Luttrell had lost the Zodiac back at the shipping lane and made his escape while visibility was reduced in the pouring rain, they now desperately needed to put as many miles as possible between Peregrine and the Zodiac.

He felt reassured that Howe's men were more likely to continue heading towards Salcombe, the original agreed destination, rather than head south towards Luttrell's present position. The most likely outcome was that they would encounter Steve heading back to Salcombe on the RIB-X. He wasn't carrying any seed and he knew nothing of what had just happened, or even the smuggling that had taken place in the past. He was innocent of it all.

Luttrell rather enjoyed the prospect of the cadaverous, intense Howe or one of his men trying to interrogate Steve as to what part he had played. He knew nothing and his reply could only be along the lines of "I drank a lot of beer and had a nice sail". Importantly, Luttrell had told Steve nothing of where he now intended to sail with Vilda.

Luttrell turned to Vilda. "Everything is going to be OK now angel. When we get to safety I will tell you all about everything that just happened, but right now we need to get a move on. Take the helm and head south west. I need to go down below and get the long range weather forecast and work out our route. We are heading for the Mediterranean, final destination Mallorca!"

Vilda smiled and as the yacht bore off to the correct heading, Luttrell checked the trim of the sails before descending the steps into the saloon below. He switched on the chartplotter and computer. Luttrell considered what he knew about the journey they would now have to make. To get to Mallorca from The Channel was one hell of a trip, a really long voyage of ten days or more that would involve crossing the notorious Bay of Biscay in order to get from the northern coast of France to the northern coast of Spain.

Biscay is feared by yachtsmen because of the often gale force winds and huge waves rolling unbroken across the Atlantic until hitting the shallower waters of the continental shelf rising in the Bay itself. In severe conditions, the wind is usually from a westerly direction and drives boats onto the rocky coastland, the only ports being too dangerous to escape into if the wind or waves are high.

The sailor faces two options: Hug the coast and hope that the weather is relatively fine or head way offshore towards the Canary Islands, missing the worst of the conditions in the Bay of Biscay, before taking a dog leg turn south east towards the mouth of the Mediterranean Sea.

The latter being the traditional route - a long, lonely sail in true offshore conditions. It was the route taken by square riggers in the past who didn't have the benefit of a long range weather forecast to reassure them that the wind and waves wouldn't drive their boats onto the rocky coast.

Luttrell checked the five day weather forecast. It was early August and the forecast was for relatively light winds over the next few days. However a gale had recently blown itself out in the Atlantic and the swell was expected to be rough, uncomfortable but manageable. There were likely to be some scattered rain showers, but nothing too serious.

Steve had fully provisioned the boat and there was no-one else Luttrell would prefer to be holed up with on a long arduous sail than the lovely blonde Viking currently singing something off-key in impenetrable Swedish as she helmed the boat. They would take the traditional route, at times hundreds of miles offshore, and use the time and space to plan their future together. They would be hidden offshore for a couple of days, answerable to no-one and independent from the rest of the mad, bad world.

Luttrell heard a shriek from on deck and rushed up the companionway steps to see Vilda pointing at something in the water near the boat. There were dolphins all around the hull, glinting silver as they raced by onto some unknown destination. Vilda turned and smiled, wide-eyed with childish enthusiasm.

CHAPTER 20

The finca was on a hill a couple of hundred metres above the port of Pollenca, in the north of Mallorca. A traditional Iberian farmhouse built of rose-coloured stone sitting in the middle of a rolling valley filled with olive trees and lemon groves. A long driveway wound its way through the fragrant trees to a tall set of electronic wooden gates and substantial stone walling, blocking any view of the property from the public road. There were no other buildings in the valley and their two dogs, scruffy mongrels from a rescue shelter, had the run of the place, barking furiously at the merest hint of outsiders.

Luttrell lay naked on the bed, looking out of the open french windows at the sea glistening in the sunlight, a mile or so away. His deeply tanned skin a sharp contrast to the fresh white bed linen. A light breeze carried the fragrance from the lemon grove and toyed with the billowing drapes, cooling the room. Vilda was taking a shower.

They had done it. Three years of smuggling and adventure. Escaping threatened prosecution and achieving the total disruption of an evil plan that would have resulted in slaughter, pandemic and suffering on a truly global scale. The Athena Mechanism broken, fractured, prevented from achieving the politicians' nefarious aims.

An arduous sail across the Bay of Biscay, south along Portugal's coast and then through the Pillars of Hercules into the Mediterranean Sea. Their money waiting for them in the Spanish bank account.

Luttrell lit a cigarette and reflected on having everything that he had ever wanted.

Peregrine was berthed in the busy marina at the nearby port and used regularly, along with another smaller yacht that they had purchased, for excursions by the sailing school that Luttrell had set up shortly after they had purchased the finca. Tourists were taught the basics of sailing, or just taken out for a day trip to a nearby bay, by the rugged Englishman and his blonde, smiling Swedish partner. No-one really knew much about them, they just seemed to have turned up from nowhere one day.

There were rumours amongst the other sailing instructors of long boat trips to mainland Spain, always leaving or arriving at night time, and whispers of smuggling but the locals dismissed such scurrilous rumours with a shrug of the shoulders and attributed them to be the products of envy and jealous minds. It was nobody's business but their own.

ABOUT THE AUTHOR

Thornton was born in Birmingham, England in 1971 and is a qualified lawyer. Thornton currently resides in Hereford, UK and writes fiction and non-fiction titles. An interest in politics and a healthy suspicion of authority figures inform his work.

Thornton owns a boat which is used as frequently as the British weather allows, often with his two children.

A member of The Freedom Association and The Law Society of England and Wales.

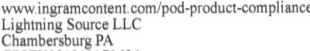